"May I ask wh
doing in my garden?"

Oh, no! Not him! Candy's spirits sank. Marshall Scott—famous photographer and local celebrity—frowned in a depressingly familiar way.

"Do I know you?" he asked.

"Well, we haven't been introduced or anything, but we did meet yesterday at the fete." Candy reached out a hand, then realized that if Marshall Scott came close enough to shake it, his dog would come close, too.

"Candy Harper," she went on lamely, as she pulled her hand back. "I don't expect you remember. I was the fortune-teller, the—the Chinese Oracle."

Her voice faded away as it dawned on her that this confession was not at all likely to endear her to Mr. Scott. And his thunderous look confirmed her fears.

"How could I forget?" he said bleakly.

SALLY COOK lives in Norwich with her two small sons. She was a professional writer for nine years before she branched into romance fiction.

Books by Sally Cook

HARLEQUIN PRESENTS

1223—DEEP HARBOUR
1287—BELONGING
1320—HIJACKED HEART

SALLY COOK

tiger's tail

Harlequin Books

TORONTO • NEW YORK • LONDON
AMSTERDAM • PARIS • SYDNEY • HAMBURG
STOCKHOLM • ATHENS • TOKYO • MILAN

Harlequin Presents first edition November 1991
ISBN 0-373-11407-9

Original hardcover edition published in 1990
by Mills & Boon Limited

TIGER'S TAIL

Printed in U.S.A.

CHAPTER ONE

'WHEN a blade of grass is pulled up,' Candy Harper read out loud, 'it brings with it other blades which are attached to it. Advancing will be fortunate.'

'Grass? Grass? What's grass got to do with my question?'

'Well, it's an oracle, Mrs Watson. You don't have to take it literally. You need to think about it until it makes sense to you. Maybe it means that if you take a stand over the storm drains, the rest of the Parish Council will support you. You make the first move—you pull up your piece of grass—and they'll have to come with you. Because they're attached to you, just as in a clump of grass all the roots are intertwined, and you can't pull out one blade on its own.'

Mrs Watson, fat, cheerful and fiftyish, threw back her head and laughed.

'What a faradiddle!' she chortled. 'Blades of grass, indeed! Sounds to me like you could make it mean anything you wanted.'

'Not quite anything,' Candy protested. 'It's true, though, that it can mean many things. In a way that's part of the value of it. It reflects your subconscious mind, helps you see what you really want to do.'

'Load of twaddle, lovey. But you've given me a laugh, and it's all in a good cause. And I do like your outfit, you've done yourself up a treat.'

'Thanks, Mrs Watson.'

'Any time, lovey.' Mrs Watson deposited her thirty pence on the table in front of Candy, and raised herself, heavily, from her chair.

After Mrs Watson had gone Candy got up herself, reached outside, and swung round the sign on the tent flap so it announced that the Chinese Oracle was 'Available for Consultation'.

Mrs Watson had been a perfect client. Jokey, good-humoured, she had also been interested in what the Oracle had to say, and willing to half believe in it. Most of Candy's customers had reacted in much the same way.

Poor Oracle, Candy thought, glancing at the square of black silk on which rested her book in its black cover and three silver coins. Treating it in this way wasn't doing justice to its three-thousand-year-old wisdom. She was raising a handy few pounds for the village hall fund, though. Only once or twice, between customers, had she thought that it might have been more enjoyable out in the open air where she could have nattered with passers-by and with the other stallholders.

Come on, next customer, she thought silently. She glanced at her watch. Four-thirty: two hours since the fête had opened. Little Bixton wasn't a large village and, though Juliet had told her the fête always drew a reasonable crowd, she hadn't expected to have a queue outside her tent. It had been flattering to have one for the first hour or so, but now the customers were coming more and more slowly.

She heard voices as a couple of people approached the tent, and then made them out to be customers from earlier in the day, so she wasn't too disappointed when they passed on without disturbing her. Then it was quiet for a while. In the distance, the loudspeaker was announcing that the Under-Sevens' Fancy Dress would be judged in five minutes.

Maybe I should go and look at the under-sevens, Candy thought. After all, in two weeks' time I'll be teaching some of them. Then she heard more voices: a man and a woman, arguing just outside the tent.

'Oh, come on, Marshall,' the woman was saying. 'Do have a go. It's great fun, really it is. I did it earlier, and absolutely everybody else has.'

That's Caroline Greenwood, Candy thought. She had met Caroline a couple of days before, a statuesque blonde whose father ran a large farm just outside the village. Who was Marshall? Caroline's boyfriend, presumably.

'You know I don't believe in that sort of rubbish,' the man retorted.

'You don't have to believe in it, for heaven's sake! It's supposed to be a joke, though she does it very well, actually. It's Juliet Snowdon's sister. She's only just moved into the village.'

'It's not a joke, Caroline,' Marshall persisted. 'I regard all this kind of thing as pernicious rubbish. Horoscopes and crystal balls and palmistry, it's all stupid and dangerous and I won't encourage it.'

'Oh, you stick-in-the-mud! Only you could get all high and mighty about a fortune teller's tent at a village fête! Can't you ever learn to take a joke, Marshall?'

'I can enjoy plenty of jokes, but this isn't one of them!'

'Rubbish! You're the most humourless man I've ever met!'

There was a scuffling sound, as if Caroline was underlining her point by marching away. Then Marshall's voice, shouting, 'Caroline...' and then the pair of them seemed to have moved right out of earshot.

Candy's spirits fell a little. She could have done with at least one more customer before she called it a day. Still, she told herself, it didn't sound as if having Marshall as a customer would have been much fun.

She picked up the coins and chinked them idly in her hand, wondering whether she could reasonably pack up now, or whether she ought to hang on till five o'clock. Perhaps Juliet or Peter, Juliet's husband, would come back soon and tell her.

The tent flap was suddenly thrust open, and a man stalked in.

'I warn you,' he announced, without making any move to sit down, 'I don't approve of all this.'

Both the words and the newly familiar voice made it evident that this was Marshall. Instinctively Candy glanced behind him, to see if Caroline would follow him in and stand in triumph over him while the Oracle had its say. Obviously she took her victories more coolly, though, because there was no sign of her.

Candy turned her attention back to Marshall, and gave him her sweetest smile.

'Don't you? That's good. I always like sceptical customers. It's such fun to see the expression on their faces when the Oracle gets it right.'

'Rubbish,' Marshall retorted. 'Oracles can't "get it right", except by coincidence. It's impossible.'

'Can't they?' Candy gazed up at him: a long way up, because he was tall. It wasn't easy to tell how tall when she was sitting, but she reckoned he was perhaps a foot more than her own five feet two. He was slim but broad-shouldered, and casually dressed in dark trousers and an open-necked striped shirt. He looked to be several years older than Caroline: perhaps thirty, or even thirty-five. His hair was dark, shortish and curly, and as far as she could tell in the gloom of the tent—just one strategically placed torch lit up her table—he was rather good-looking.

Lucky Caroline, she thought for a minute. Or perhaps not so lucky, if he really was such a humourless brute.

'All the same,' she went on, 'it won't hurt, I promise. And that's better than the dentist's promise any day! Won't you sit down?'

Marshall stood there for a moment more, as if he was going to refuse. Candy didn't let herself show any impatience. He had come into the tent, after all; she was willing to bet he would go through with it now.

Finally he stirred, pulled out the chair Mrs Watson had vacated, and sat in it, bringing himself into the range of the torch beam.

As the light brought his face into focus, Candy found herself revising her opinion. No, he wasn't rather good-looking: he was *very* good-looking. His face was almost classic in its perfection, though there was something about the high, angular cheekbones that added a certain individuality to it. He had a long narrow nose, straight brows, a widish mouth, and deep-set eyes that looked almost black in the gloom of the tent. Definitely the type to earn a second look from her—or from any other woman between fifteen and ninety-five, come to that!

He might be a sour old grouch, but even scowling he was devastatingly attractive. While if he were to smile . . . well, she'd make him smile, or even laugh, before she was through with him!

She bestowed on him another of her own best smiles, and tried not to take it amiss when he didn't respond to it in the slightest.

'Do you know anything about the I Ching, Mr...'

'Scott. No, and I don't want to. Just do it as fast as you can.'

'OK. Well, all you absolutely have to know, Mr Scott, is that the I Ching doesn't tell fortunes in the general sense. It gives advice based on questions that it's asked. So before I can do anything you have to think of a question to ask the Oracle.'

'I see.' Marshall Scott was silent for a moment. His eyes lowered to the paraphernalia on the table, and his brows seemed to move together, almost imperceptibly. Then he looked up again at Candy and said, 'All right, I'm ready.'

'Then could you tell me your question, please?'

'No.'

'No?'

'No.' Marshall Scott held her eyes. He smiled. Just as ordered. Well, not quite as ordered: it wasn't a very friendly smile, there was a positively sardonic edge to it.

But it had quite an effect on her, even so. A little trickle of awareness seemed to slide down her spine. Gosh, he was gorgeous! He might be rude and arrogant and humourless, but it would almost be worth putting up with all that for the sheer pleasure of looking at him.

She wasn't here to look, though. She was here to tell his fortune. And curse him, he wasn't playing ball!

In fact, he was playing dirty. He was smiling, damn him, knowing just what effect that smile must have on every woman who set eyes on him, and he was refusing to tell her his question, knowing that it would keep her from bluffing her way through the fortune-telling even if the oracle's answer didn't make a blind bit of sense. In short, he was setting her up to go ahead and make a thorough fool of herself.

His eyes left hers. She watched them travel from her hair, slicked back into a long pigtail, down to Juliet's old kimono, on to the book and coins laid out on the table, and back to her own eyes with their heavy black eyeliner.

It wasn't a smile on his face now, it was a smirk. Don't you look idiotic? it seemed to say. Nothing gorgeous about you, is there? In fact, you look an absolute sight.

Curse him! She had had enough put-downs from arrogant men to last several lifetimes already! She wasn't going to let them get to her. Hadn't she told herself that? All that was behind her, as far behind as Andrew and London.

So what if you don't like what you see, Mr Marshall Scott? she thought furiously to herself. Somehow we'll get one over on you, me and my Oracle!

Marshall Scott might be a particularly awkward customer, but she knew just how to deal with awkward customers. She had had plenty of practice with stubborn five-year-olds. And, though he might not believe in it, she herself really did reckon that the Oracle worked. She had been dabbling with it for several months, and her feeling was that much of the time the answers it gave *were* relevant, amazingly so considering that it had been created by a totally different race and society.

Laugh her way through it? No, not this time! She would play it straight down the line, and trust the Oracle to come up with the goods.

'You do *have* a question?'

'Yes, I do.'

'Then hold it clearly in your mind, and take the three coins.'

Marshall picked them up and looked at them.

'Are these ancient Chinese talismans?'

'No, they're ten-pence pieces.'

'Oh, very ancient and oracular!'

'It's not the equipment that counts, it's the spirit in which you do it. Now think hard about your question, shake the coins, and throw them, all at once, so they land on the piece of silk.'

To her relief he did this without comment. She leaned over, and checked the coins. Tails three times: an Old Yin line.

'Now what?'

'Do it five more times.'

Marshall threw. He kept a faintly sceptical look on his face, but at least he did what she had told him. Candy noted down the results of each throw: Young Yin, Young Yang, Young Yang.

'Right,' she said, when she had written down the last one. 'Now to find out what the Oracle has to tell you.'

'What do I get? One cryptic clue?'

'No, there's more than that. These six throws make up a hexagram, a pattern of six lines. See? Each different hexagram has a name, and there's a different pronouncement for each one. Some of the lines in the pattern also have special commentaries. Then you transform the pattern into a second hexagram which sheds extra light on your question. There's quite a lot to take in.'

'It sounds thoroughly confusing to me.'

'There's no need for you to understand all the technicalities. I'll tell you what the Oracle says. If I knew what your question was, I could interpret it for you too.'

'But you don't, do you?'

'How true.'

'Anyway, I dare say it's all so ambiguous that it won't make any sense to me at all.'

'Oh, I wouldn't say that,' Candy said. 'It's—it's strange, as you'll see. Obviously it can't answer your question precisely, but sometimes it's quite specific.' She opened her book at the chart listing all the hexagrams and their names, and traced her finger down and across the rows and columns.

'The top three lines make a pattern called *"Tui"*: that stands for joyfulness. The bottom three make a pattern called *"Ken"*, the immovable. Together, they produce a hexagram called . . .'

How awful! she thought, as her eyes stopped on the name. Or—how wonderful, if only she could keep her cool and milk it for all it was worth! If anything would embarrass this supercilious, arrogant man, that would!

'It's a hexagram called *"Hsien"*. That translates into English, more or less, as "Mutual Attraction".'

'Mutual attraction?'

Candy fought to quell the grin that was trying to erupt. Oh, the astonishment in his voice! It wouldn't do to tease him, though. Then he might think she was flirting with him, and that would be humiliating.

The mutual attraction wasn't between the two of them. That was too obvious to be worth thinking about. The only attraction there was definitely one-way only. But she didn't have to look far to track down a convincing example of the phenomenon.

Why had he come to have his fortune told? Because Caroline Greenwood had nagged him into doing it.

Beautiful blonde Caroline was the last person he had seen before he came into the tent. So what would he think of, if he had to think up a question on the spur of the moment?

Was it conceivable? Was it possible? No, it was more than that: it was *probable* that he had asked about Caroline. She didn't want to spoil the effect by suggesting that to him: but then she wouldn't need to, because he would surely see for himself that the I Ching was spot-on.

'Here it is,' she said, flattening the page as she set the book down on the table, and twisting it towards him so he could read it too. 'This is The Decision, set down by a Chinese ruler called Wen in the year 1143 BC: "Mutual Attraction. Firm correctness will lead to success. There is advantage in marrying a young girl. There will be good fortune." '

'Good fortune in marriage? Rubbish!'

'That's what it says,' Candy retorted, glancing up at Marshall and giving him a wicked grin. 'There's more to come.' She turned the book a little further towards him, and angled it under the light so they could both read the paragraphs that followed.

' "The superior man keeps his mind free from all preoccupations, and is open to receive the approaches of all who come to him," ' Marshall read out.

'The superior man can be you, you see, if you follow the natural rhythms of nature. "I Ching" means "The Book of Changes"; it's all about doing the right things at the right time. You could say that here it's telling you off for being sceptical about its teachings.'

'Could you?'

'Well, *I* could. Then we go on to the individual lines, and you have to read the verdict on the first line, here.'

'"He wriggles his toes"?'

'True, that is a bit cryptic. There's a commentary to explain, though, written by Confucius or one of his followers. See: "However much a man may wriggle his toes, it will not enable him to walk. Intentions are not enough: action must follow."'

'That's it?'

'No, then we transform the hexagram by changing this first line, and we get another hexagram. Which is'—another fumble through the charts—*"Ko"*, or "Revolution". "Revolution is only believed in when it has been accomplished. There will be great progress and success. Advantage will come from being firm and correct, removing all occasion for regret."'

'"Occasion for regret",' Marshall echoed.

'That's a favourite phrase of the I Ching. It's full of formula phrases with special meanings. The superior man; being firm and correct; having occasion for regret; all this comes up again and again.'

'So I'd have had much the same answer whatever throws I made?'

'Oh, no. Look through them if you like, and judge for yourself if any of the other hexagrams would have fitted your question.'

Marshall didn't reply, or take her up on this offer. Candy stared at him. He wasn't looking at her now: his eyes were fixed on the book.

It *was* apt, she thought. He's not going to back down and admit it, but it has made sense to him. I must have been right: he did ask about Caroline. The Oracle's answer could hardly have been more accurate, could it? Any idiot could tell that those two are made for each other. Caroline is so beautiful in her cool blonde way, and Marshall is so handsome in his smouldering dark way. I bet they just drool every time they see each other.

Mind, he didn't like the bit about marriage. Maybe Caroline is already trying to tie him down, and he's fighting shy of the commitment. It serves him right, though: he asked the Oracle what he should do, and he got a clear answer.

How funny, she thought with an inward tickle of amusement. Marshall Scott had been the most sceptical customer she had had all afternoon, but she suspected that the Oracle's message had hit home better with him than with any of the others. Maybe it was because her own annoyance with him had in some mysterious way fuelled the Oracle to perform at its peak. Maybe it was simply because he hadn't expected it. He hadn't been looking for a scrap of fortune-telling that he could twist to fit his own requirements, he had been convinced before he started that the message he received would be irrelevant to him.

From his silence and his frown, she judged that he couldn't decide what to think, let alone what to say. Would he admit he had been wrong about the Oracle? Would he tell her now what his question had been?

Not a chance, she decided, taking in the thin line of his mouth and his lowered brows. Marshall Scott looked to be a man of fixed opinions, and it would take more than one lucky shot to change his attitude to fortune-telling. Without a doubt he was also the kind of man who kept his personal life to himself. It was too much to hope that he would admit to her that the Oracle had surprised him, and pretty inconceivable that he would discuss with her the pros and cons of marrying Caroline Greenwood.

Nor did she particularly want him to, if she was honest. She had her little victory over him, but somehow it didn't taste as sweet as she had intended. He had stirred up too many uncomfortable feelings, too many unhappy memories. Will-power alone couldn't take away the hurt that Andrew had inflicted, couldn't give back the self-confidence that he had destroyed so thoroughly. Alone and uncertain, she wasn't yet able to look on other people's love-affairs with the unselfish delight that she would have wished to feel. Watching handsome Marshall deliberate over lovely Caroline was a sour-edged pleasure, when you were plain Candy with nobody thinking about you at all.

'That'll be thirty pence, please,' she said instead.

Marshall looked up at her. He blinked, as if his thoughts had been far away.

'Oh. Yes.' He fumbled in his pockets, and brought out a pound coin.

'I'll just find you some change.'

'No need,' said Marshall. When Candy looked up, with seventy pence ready in her hand, he had already left the tent.

Candy's next visitor was Juliet, looking harassed, and dragging a protesting two-year-old Patrick behind her.

'All finished,' Juliet said, dumping Patrick on the customer's chair. 'Can I leave Patrick with you while I go and see to packing up the Wheel of Fortune?'

'Of course. Hey, Patrick, want to be my helper while I count up my takings?'

Patrick didn't answer. 'Thanks,' his mother said. 'The money goes to Mrs Lichford, the tall woman in blue who was running the Tombola. Giles and Mr Smith will be over soon to take the tent down, so you don't have to worry about that.' Juliet patted Patrick's shoulder, and disappeared in a rush.

Candy and Patrick got to work, totting up piles of ten-pence and twenty-pence pieces. Five pounds twenty. That added up to fifteen customers at thirty pence each, plus Marshall Scott's overpayment at the end of the afternoon. It was hardly a fortune for an afternoon's work. Maybe she should have charged more. It had been a good giggle, though, and made her a few new acquaintances in the village. The Tombola and some of the other stalls would have done much better, but it took a balance of attractions to make a success of a village fête, and several people had congratulated her on her originality.

Candy would have been happy to collapse back at her cottage when the clearing up was over, but Juliet insisted that she come round for supper. That made sense, anyway. Bell Cottage was frankly a mess. In the two weeks since she had moved in the woodworm had been treated, the walls injected with damp-proofing, and the sad apology for a kitchen in the open-plan downstairs demolished. The whole place stank of chemicals, and there wasn't anywhere to cook supper, unless you counted a tiny camping-gas stove.

So she stopped only to wipe away the Chinese make-up, untie her pigtail and brush her hair, and change her clothes for a more conventional skirt and T-shirt. Then she set off down the village street.

Little Bixton boasted two churches—St Margaret's and a nonconformist chapel—a junior school, a post office, a pub, the Poacher's Pocket, and a small row of shops. All these sprawled around the village green, a triangular patch of grass with a tiny muddy pond in the middle, together with a couple of rows of small terraced cottages. Cottages also lined the intersecting streets that converged on St Margaret's Church, and on the outskirts of the village were an assortment of larger houses, one of which housed Peter and Juliet.

Candy had been visiting Little Bixton to see Juliet for years, but until Juliet had phoned to tell her about a vacancy for a teacher in the junior school she had never thought of moving there herself. She had been a Londoner all her life. Then suddenly the village had seemed like the right place at the right time. She hadn't had any reason to stay in London after Andrew had told her he was leaving her for Georgina, and the job had been just what she was looking for.

Everything had seemed to fall into place. She had inherited a small legacy from her great-aunt and she had been lucky enough to find Bell Cottage, semi-ruinous admittedly, but cheap enough for her to afford, and situated on the green just a minute's walk from the school.

But I mustn't get into the habit of going to supper at Juliet's too often, she thought as she made her way past the Poacher's Pocket and down Smugglers' Row. She and Peter have their own friends to see, and I'll need to make some of my own. It's a pity there aren't more single people in Little Bixton. Perhaps I'll make friends with Caroline Greenwood.

She found Juliet in the kitchen. Patrick was already asleep, and supper half prepared.

'Can I help?'

'No, all fixed. We'll eat in ten minutes. The fête did really well, broke all records. We made eight hundred and forty-two pounds, fifty-seven pence.'

'That's wonderful. Mind, my little effort didn't contribute much.'

'It went down very well,' Peter said, coming into the kitchen with a glass of sherry in each hand, and delivering one to each of the sisters. 'Lots of people said how different it was.'

'That's not always a compliment,' Candy retorted with a laugh.

'It was, from most of them,' Juliet said. 'Though you must be careful not to get a reputation for being too way-out, Candy.'

Candy smiled, unconcernedly. What a typically Juliet thing to say! Juliet had always been conventionally minded, always fussed and worried whenever Candy's clothes or her behaviour didn't fit her own narrow preconceptions.

'Carl Jung believed in the I Ching,' she responded.

'Jung could afford to,' Peter said.

And I can't? How unreasonable! she thought. Then the memory came of Marshall Scott's forthrightly expressed disapproval; and following hard on its heels she recalled the raised eyebrows of Mrs Kipling, the headmistress of the little village school.

Maybe Peter and Juliet were right. She was new to the village, and almost as new to being a teacher; she couldn't afford to gain a reputation for being weird. Joking was all right, but it might be as well not to let people think that she took the Oracle too seriously.

Juliet dished up dinner, and they ate their carrot soup in silence. Then there was a pause as Juliet grilled the steaks.

'You might call it coincidence,' Candy said, 'but the I Ching did turn up some extraordinary answers this afternoon.'

'Like what?' Juliet turned, put her hands together and bowed her head, and intoned, 'You will meet a tall, dark, handsome stranger. You will marry him. You will have sixteen children.'

Candy and Peter both laughed.

'Actually,' Candy said, 'I did meet a tall, dark, handsome stranger. I told his fortune, but the Oracle advised him to marry someone else.'

'Did it? How thoughtless of it,' Juliet said, as she ladled the food on to their plates. 'Who was he? Any idea? Little Bixton isn't exactly overflowing with stunning men.'

'Well, this one was devastating,' Candy said cheerfully. 'Right in the tradition of Heathcliff and Mr Rochester, all smouldering resentment and short-fuse passion. But he's spoken for, as far as I could tell, and he was a bit supercilious for my taste.'

'Oh, you mean Marshall Scott,' Peter said.

'Marshall Scott?' Juliet echoed. 'Oh, of course! As if I could forget about Marshall Scott! Come to think, Mrs Kipling commented about his turning up.'

'Doesn't he usually?' Candy asked, curious.

'Not generally,' Juliet said. 'Wouldn't you say, Peter?'

'Not in the Poacher's Pocket,' Peter agreed. 'Hardly ever. He's the sort who'll always dish out a cheque when the vicar duns him, but he's not the kind to join the village darts team, and he doesn't often turn up at local charity "do"s either. I suppose our Marshall's got bigger fish to fry.'

'Our Marshall?' Candy echoed, intrigued.

'You've heard of Marshall Scott, surely, Candy?'

'Why, should I have?'

'I thought everybody had,' Juliet said, with mock sadness at this realisation that Marshall Scott's fame hadn't spread as far as she had thought. 'He's our great local celebrity, Candy. Marshall Scott, the famous photographer.'

CHAPTER TWO

CANDY was up by half-past seven the next morning, even though it was Sunday. Once she was caught up in the routine of teaching there would be hardly any time to put her cottage to rights, so she couldn't afford to waste a moment of the holidays.

Bell Cottage *could* be charming, she was sure, but oh, there was a lot of work to be done before it was! And most of it would have to be done by her, since her budget was too tight to pay builders' fees. She was starting today with the self-assembly cupboards she had bought for the kitchen.

She slipped on a very old, paint-stained pair of denims and a big shirt that had once been Peter's, tied her long brown hair back in a pony-tail, downed a cup of coffee, ate a slice of toast and butter, and set to work on the mountain of flatpack cartons.

Ten minutes later she was puffing and despairing. Never mind assembling the units, it was almost more than she could do to get the cartons open! Her fingernails were broken, and a big blister was coming up between her thumb and forefinger. She made another cup of coffee, switched on her radio to cheer herself up, and started again.

This time she fared a little better, but it was ten o'clock by the time she had all the cartons open. Then actually assembling the cupboards proved a little easier, but not much. It seemed to take incredible amounts of wrenching and heaving to make fittings fit where they were supposed to.

At one o'clock she dunked herself quickly under the shower and nipped round to the Poacher's Pocket to buy two rounds of ham sandwiches with mustard and half a pint of bitter. Then it was back to work.

By mid-afternoon, she was weary and lonely and feeling thoroughly fed-up. Juliet and Peter wouldn't call round because they had set off that morning to visit Peter's parents. She barely knew any other people in the village, so she couldn't expect other visitors, but it was depressing to think that except for the quick trip to the pub she had seen nobody all day.

Her arms were aching powerfully, but she couldn't afford to stop yet. In the morning the village's jobbing builder, Mr Watson, would come to install her new sink, hob, cooker and washing-machine. She had to have the floor cupboards at least fitted before then. She sighed and picked up her hammer again.

There was a particularly awkward place where the sink was to go. A water pipe seemed to run precisely where she wanted to fix a batten. She lodged the wood just beneath the pipe, and tapped. Dongggg! The hammer hit the pipe. Careful, Candy, she told herself.

Tap, tap, tap, dongggg! Another awkward miss. Gently, now. She shifted on her heels, and tapped more cautiously.

The nail was going in now. Just a few more good hard . . .

Thungggg! Candy let go of the nail and reached out to stop the length of pipe vibrating.

It was wet.

Oh, no, she hadn't holed it! She dropped the hammer and leaned forward, and a sudden rush of water hit her straight in the face, knocking her backwards on to the hard concrete floor.

She soon recovered from the shock of it, and a few minutes later she had managed to turn off the water supply and stop the gushing water. But not soon enough! Everything was soaked: the cupboard doors, the frames, her tools, the floor, Candy herself.

She jumped up, spraying water everywhere, and let out one loud exasperated howl! Then she began to heave the pieces of wood out of the huge puddle on the floor, and mop it up.

She had handled the crisis pretty well, she thought to herself as she squeezed the mop out for absolutely the last time. But oh, boy, did she have problems! The cupboards were still hours away from being finished, she felt shattered, and she couldn't possibly mend the pipe herself. Nor would she have any running water in the cottage until it was mended.

She needed help from Mr Watson the builder and plumber, and she needed it right away, even though it was almost five-thirty on a summer Sunday afternoon.

It was only a minute's dash across the street to the Watsons' cottage. But when she got there she found that Mr Watson wasn't in.

'He's up at Little Bixton Hall, dear,' Mrs Watson told her. 'Been working there all afternoon.'

'Maybe I could telephone him there? I really do need him urgently.'

'Let me see, dear.' Mrs Watson reached for the phone book, and flicked through the pages. She frowned.

'Oh, silly me. Mr Scott only moved in a month or two back. The number's probably listed under the Major's name still.'

There was a number under the Major's name, but when Mrs Watson rang it, she got a 'disconnected' tone.

'Let's try directory enquiries,' Candy suggested.

They did. But there was no number listed for any Scotts in Little Bixton.

'He's probably ex-directory, lovey,' Mrs Watson said. 'That'd be just like Mr Scott. Likes to keep to himself, he does.'

'What can I do? Are there any other plumbers in the village?'

'Not this side of Wansham, love, and the Wansham plumbers charge a fortune for Sunday call-outs. Why don't you pop on up to the Hall? It won't take you ten minutes.'

'Whereabout is it?'

'Up Whiskey Lane, past Bates' farm on the left. You can't miss it.'

'Is it far?'

'Maybe a mile and a half: walking distance. You watch those wet trousers, though. You'll chafe your legs for certain if you go in them, and most likely give yourself a proper chill. Why don't you nip back home and change first?'

'No time!' Candy cried, escaping from Mrs Watson's friendly concern and dashing up the street towards Whiskey Lane.

As Mrs Watson had said, you couldn't miss Little Bixton Hall. It was huge, a gracious country mansion in mellow redbrick, early Georgian from the look of it, with rows of perfectly aligned sash windows. Dead centre, an elegantly curved double staircase led up to a massive front door.

Candy stopped and stared at this imposing entrance. It was rather too imposing, she decided, for someone coming on her kind of errand, and in soaked and filthy working clothes. She would do better to hunt out a tradesman's entrance. There would be one at the back somewhere, she supposed.

From either side of the house a brick wall stretched out, but there was a door in it just by the far wall of the house. Candy walked up to this and knocked. Would anyone hear her knocking on an outside door? She doubted it. When nobody came in five minutes, she tried the latch. It opened easily.

On the other side, a brick-paved path led down the side of the house towards a formal-looking garden. Candy called out, but there was no sign of life, so she set off down the path.

She had only taken a dozen steps when she heard a bark. And another. A guard dog? Perhaps this wasn't such a good idea. She took a step backwards, then turned and took two more steps. She was about to break into a run when the dog reached her.

It was a big Alsatian. Candy backed against the house wall, and put her hands out in front of her. To her immense relief the dog stopped a pace away.

'Good dog,' she said in a shaky voice.

The dog growled.

'Good dog,' Candy repeated. Her teeth were chattering. What on earth should she do? Run for it? Shout? I'll count to five, she thought, then open my mouth and yell.

One, two, three . . .

'Blitzen!'

The dog turned. It opened its mouth, displaying sharp teeth and a panting tongue.

'Here, Blitzen.'

The dog padded off quietly towards where a man was standing at the back corner of the house. He was silhouetted against the late afternoon sun, and Candy could only see the shape of him, tall and black. His pose, with hands set on his hips and legs apart, suggested aggression. But at least she would be able to speak to him, reason with him, which was more than she could have done with the dog.

The man reached down and tucked a hand into Blitzen's collar. Then he moved forwards towards Candy, all the time holding the dog at his side.

He stopped a little further away than Blitzen had done originally.

'May I ask what you imagine you are doing in my garden?'

Oh, no! Not him! Candy's spirits sank right down into her sodden sneakers. Of course, Mr Scott! Mrs Watson had mentioned the name, but in her panic it had never occurred to her that Mr Scott was *him*.

'Er—hello, Mr Scott.'

Marshall Scott—the famous photographer and great local celebrity—frowned in a depressingly familiar way.

'Do I know you?'

'Well, we haven't been introduced or anything, but we did meet yesterday. At the fête.' Candy reached out a hand, then realised that, if Marshall Scott came close enough to shake it, the dog Blitzen would come closer too, and let it fall again. 'Candy Harper,' she went on lamely. 'I don't expect you remember. I was the fortune teller. The—the Chinese Oracle.'

Her voice faced away as it dawned on her with appalling clarity that this confession was not at all likely to endear her to Mr Scott. As it evidently didn't, to judge from the thunderous look on his face.

'How could I forget?' he said bleakly.

'It's no wonder you didn't recognise me. I mean, yesterday I had on that silly costume, and . . .'

'And today you are looking entirely different,' Marshall Scott finished for her. His eyes travelled over her. Candy knew just what he was seeing. Her hair was straggling out of its makeshift pony-tail. Her shirt was filthy, sweaty and disgusting, and her denims were thick with a muddy mixture of sawdust, plaster dust and good old-fashioned grime.

Marshall Scott, curse him, was wearing spotless and well-tailored brown trousers, and a cream short-sleeved shirt. He looked cool and composed and just as damnably handsome as she remembered.

'So I am,' she muttered.

'I take it you haven't come to tell my fortune?'

'Oh, no. Of course not. I've—well, actually, I've come to find Mr Watson.'

'Mr Watson?'

'The plumber. The builder. I need him urgently.'

'Oh, you mean Jack,' Marshall Scott said.

'Jack, then. Jack Watson.'

'I don't think he's finished yet.'

'Frankly,' Candy said, with a sudden unwise surge of temper, 'I don't care whether he's finished or not. I need him urgently.'

'Well *I* need him urgently too. And since he's already here and working for me, I'm afraid you'll have to look elsewhere for a plumber to do your urgent work.'

Blitzen let out a low growl at this point, and Marshall Scott moved a step nearer, as if he was about to escort her very firmly out of his garden.

Candy steeled herself and held her ground.

'There aren't any other plumbers around here. So I'd like to talk to Mr Watson. Please.'

Marshall Scott stopped. He stared at her. Candy stared back. She tried to ignore all the quiverings that were going on in the region of her stomach. Those deep brown eyes weren't going to get to her. She couldn't afford to lose this little battle. She had beaten him once—after a fashion—and if she stuck it out, she could surely beat him again. She had to. She couldn't do without Mr Watson, she absolutely couldn't.

Damn him, couldn't he see that? Couldn't he tell that she was in desperate straits? Couldn't he have expressed some concern, or even a little polite interest in whatever had made her come dashing into his garden looking like a one-person disaster area? Oh, no, not him! All she got from him was a maddeningly superior look that appeared to be sizing her up and rating her at a flat zero on whatever scale he employed.

Slowly, Marshall Scott's frown faded. The corners of his mouth twitched.

All right, laugh at me, Mr. Scott, Candy thought furiously, clenching her fists. You laugh all you damn well like.

He didn't laugh—quite. The twitch widened slowly into a broad, broad smile.

'My God, what a sight you are!'

'Pardon me. Next time I come visiting I'll hunt out my Dior original first.'

'No need. That shirt's rather appealing in a funny kind of way. But you can't come indoors in that state. You'd better wait here.'

His free hand pressed gently down on Blitzen's back, nudging the dog back to a sitting position. 'Stay, Blitzen,' he said. His other hand released the dog's collar, and he turned to walk back around the rear of the house.

'Please don't leave the dog here with me!' Candy wailed.

Marshall Scott spun round sharply. 'Blitzen won't touch you. He's very well trained.'

'I suppose he is, but I'm scared of dogs!' And I'm cold, and wet, and tired out, and generally fed up and miserable! she felt like adding, but with a heroic effort she kept the rest of this litany to herself.

'Oh, for heaven's sake!' Marshall Scott exclaimed. 'You'd better wait in the garden-room.'

'Thank you.'

Candy waited until he had reclaimed Blitzen's collar, then she followed him and his dog round to the back of the house.

The view hit her as soon as she reached the end of the path. It was a tremendous view. With a little cry, she ran to the edge of the terrace beyond the house, and stared out at it.

She could see down across landscaped terraces, over a small copse, as far as the village itself. There was the green and the tower of St Margaret's. She could even, by squinting, make out the faded blue paint of her own front door. And on went the view, to the river beyond the village, and rolling downland even beyond that.

It was not only stunning, it was totally unexpected. She knew running up Whiskey Lane had been hard work, but she hadn't realised how steeply she was climbing, right out of the valley in which the village lay and on to the hillside beyond.

'Have you quite finished staring?'

Candy glanced guiltily at Marshall Scott. He was standing with his hands on his hips again, looking the very picture of injured impatience.

'I'm sorry. It's just such a surprise. I mean—look,' she went on enthusiastically, 'you can see the sign of the Poacher's, and the school noticeboard, and absolutely everything. It's such a lovely clear day. I hadn't realised before, I've been indoors all day. And

I hadn't known you could get a view of the village like this anywhere. Just imagine showing this to the kids. I could show them a map of the village maybe, then bring them up here, and . . . well, somewhere like here. Somewhere near here, perhaps.'

'Perhaps,' Marshall said shortly. 'The garden-room's this way.'

He waved towards a large glass and wrought-iron conservatory, then turned and strode towards it.

The glass door was open. Candy followed him through it, and into a pretty room that was awash with plants. A great vine grew up the wall and over the roof, and the sunlight filtered greenly down through the vine-leaves. A group of cane chairs, well upholstered with loose cushions in a pretty flowery print, were clustered around a glass-topped table littered with sections of the *Sunday Times*.

'I'll let Blitzen loose just inside here,' he said meaningfully. He pulled the dog through an inner door, and shut it behind him with a loud slam.

How friendly! Candy thought sarcastically. How unnecessary! Surely he didn't really imagine that I'd go wandering into his house uninvited! I'd hardly do that, even if every plumber in Sussex were inside there!

She threw herself down into one of the low cane chairs and thrust out her legs in their damp denims in front of her. Gosh, she was weary! And gosh, her denims were filthy! Most likely she was making Marshall Scott's cushions filthy too. Well, that was just too bad.

She looked around her. What a very nice conservatory it was. Lucky Mr Scott. He seemed to have absolutely everything. He was handsome *and* rich. And foully bad-tempered, and as arrogant as they came. She knew his type. Self-satisfied, selfish, with never a thought for those who weren't born to this kind of comfortable life, who had to work hard for everything they got. Everything about his manner towards her had stunk of the lord of the manor condescending to one of the local yokels. Curse him.

There was the door through which he had disappeared. It was glazed, and through the glass panel she could see the dog Blitzen, mouth open and tongue lolling. Behind him was a sitting-room furnished in a rather chilly, formal style. It looked just the kind of sitting-room Marshall Scott *would* have, spiky and uncomfortable, without a cosy armchair in sight.

But at least the garden-room was comfortable. She glanced at the *Sunday Times*. She hadn't seen a newspaper at all that day. Did she dare to pick up a section? Mr Scott would probably think that much too forward of her.

She twiddled her thumbs for five minutes, then the door opened abruptly and Marshall Scott stepped back into the conservatory.

'Down, Blitzen,' he said. 'Jack'll be another hour or so, he says, but he'll call in at your cottage on his way home.'

Candy jumped up. 'Did you tell him it's urgent?'

'He wouldn't come at all today if it weren't, would he?'

'*Very* urgent.'

Marshall Scott frowned. He leaned one slim hip against the door-frame, propped the door open with his opposite hand, and stared at her through narrowed eyes.

Candy looked defiantly back at him. Think what you like of me, Mr Scott, she thought to herself, but I'm not leaving this house until I get Mr Watson to come with me!

'Overflowing tank?'

'Burst pipe, actually.'

'A burst pipe! In the middle of summer?'

'Amazingly enough, yes! It's flooded my whole kitchen out. Care to feel my wet jeans?'

'No, thank you. Wait here.'

He shut the door again. Candy waited.

When the door finally opened again it wasn't Marshall Scott who appeared, but Jack Watson himself, in his overalls, with a bag of tools in his hand. He nodded at Candy, and made for the outer door of the garden-room. Candy followed him. Mr Watson wasn't a talkative man, but she hoped she could conclude from this that he was going to come and fix her pipes.

'Got your car with you, lass?' he asked, when they reached the driveway.

'No, I ran up.'

'Hop in the van, then.'

Mr Watson drove back down Whiskey Lane at a leisurely pace that might, Candy supposed, be a phlegmatic plumber's normal response to an emergency call. He parked outside Bell Cottage, picked up his tools again, and waited for her to unlock the door and let him in.

There was no sign of the flood. The day was still warm, and the concrete floor looked almost dry. The cupboards were dry, and everything was stacked neatly, just as Candy had left it.

She hadn't exactly lied to Marshall Scott, Candy told herself. She had picked her words carefully, that was all. And Mr Watson must know enough about pipe breaks to be able to tell that, earlier on, the flood had been all too real.

Mr Watson got to work. He replaced the holed section of pipe. He switched the water on again and tested it. At half-past seven he packed up his tools with the air of a man who would be glad to get back home.

'Thanks ever so, Mr Watson.'

'That's OK, lass,' Mr Watson said. He hesitated. 'He's a good man, Mr Scott,' he went on slowly. 'But you don't want to rub him up the wrong way too often.'

Candy thought of saying, 'You won't tell him?' But she was pretty certain Mr Watson wouldn't give her away.

'Did he really have an emergency?'

'Yup. Overflowing tank in his loft. Pipework at the Hall hasn't been looked over for years.'

'You did leave him with his water on?'

'Reckon he'll manage till the morning.'

'Well, thanks again.'

Mr Watson didn't bother to reply to this. He nodded, picked up his tool bag, and went. And Candy went straight to her bathroom, blessing the fact that her electric shower would give her instant hot water!

CHAPTER THREE

MR WATSON didn't appear on Monday morning: just as well, since Candy had been too exhausted on Sunday evening to finish off her cupboards. He had probably realised that, she thought.

She set to work again, and by midday she had all the floor cupboards finished, and the doors attached. Things were definitely going in the right direction! I'm ready for you now, Mr Watson, she thought, and decided to grab a quick bite of lunch while she waited for him to turn up. He still hadn't appeared by the time she had finished her sandwich, so she started on the wall cupboards next.

This was even harder work, since she had to manhandle the heavy cupboards into position against the walls and then fix them there. It wasn't quite impossible to do it single-handed, but it didn't seem far off impossible, especially for someone who was only five feet two! Come on, Mr Watson, Candy kept repeating to herself. But Mr Watson didn't appear.

At three o'clock Candy crossed the road and knocked on the door of his cottage. No reply. At four she knocked again. A neighbour put her head over the fence and explained that Mrs Watson didn't get back from work until five-thirty.

'What about Mr Watson?' Candy asked.

'Oh I couldn't tell you where he is, lovey.'

Well he isn't at home, thought Candy, and he isn't at Bell Cottage, Little Bixton either. She sat down on a packing case and had a think.

The answer was obvious. Instead of coming to her, Mr Watson had gone back to Little Bixton Hall.

How long did it take to mend a tank in the roof? she wondered. Not a day and a half, surely. Perhaps Mr Scott had had some other jobs to be done too. She made herself another cup of coffee and set back to work.

On Tuesday morning Candy overslept: no wonder, after two days' exhausting work. She washed and dressed hastily. Might Mr Watson have knocked and had no reply? She dashed across to his house, but it was empty.

On Wednesday she was up at seven-fifteen. When Mr Watson hadn't appeared by eight-thirty she popped across the road. The house was deserted again.

Curse Mr Watson! He couldn't still be working at Little Bixton Hall. Could he?

He could. Oh, she could believe that. He would do Marshall Scott's work before he did hers any day; not to punish her for the emergency that hadn't quite been an emergency, but simply because Marshall Scott was a bigger and more important client. But she needed him herself, needed him badly. She couldn't get on with the rest of her own work until he had done his bit. She was getting tired of doing her washing-up in a bowl on the back lawn and her cooking on the camping-gas stove.

Didn't he realise that? Maybe not, she thought pragmatically. Men didn't always understand about that kind of thing. She needed to take him aside and explain to him what terrible problems he was causing her.

She needed to go to Little Bixton Hall.

And face Marshall Scott again? Face that horrible dog? It wasn't a tempting prospect, but there really didn't seem to be any alternative, so she supposed she would have to suffer it.

She went upstairs and fished out from her wardrobe a pale blue cotton skirt and top. She changed from her painting clothes into these, ran a comb through her hair, and glanced in the mirror to make sure there were no dirty smudges on her face. None. She looked perfectly respectable. She grabbed her car keys and set off before she could have any second thoughts.

A few minutes later her little Renault was scrunching to a halt on the gravel of the hall fore-court. She got out and slammed the door, and stood for a moment looking up at the beautiful façade.

What a big house. Too big for a bachelor. A house like this needed a family to fill it. Maybe I was even more right than I suspected with my Chinese Oracle, she thought. Maybe when Marshall Scott bought it he was already thinking of marrying Caroline Greenwood. That would make sense. This would be a wonderful place to bring up children.

By the front door was an enormous brass door-knocker shaped like a lion's head. Nervously, Candy picked this up and dropped it down, then she noticed the prosaic electric doorbell just above it, so she rang that as well.

She waited for several minutes, then she heard the muffled sound of footsteps.

A middle-aged woman in a flowery apron cau-tiously opened the door to her.

'Good morning,' Candy said brightly. 'Is Mr Scott in?'

'You're late. He's been getting impatient.' The woman left the door ajar, and disappeared back into the house.

Mr Scott, impatient? What's new? Candy thought. If Mr Scott ever had pleasant moods, she certainly hadn't seen any sign of them. Better gear herself up for another tricky confrontation.

Oh, curse it! Of course, she could have asked the woman for Mr Watson, and avoided seeing Marshall Scott at all. How stupid of her. She should have thought of that sooner. It was too late now.

'You're nearly an hour late,' Marshall Scott announced, flinging the door wide open.

Candy gulped. He looked so tall and forbidding. He was only a pace away from her, and he was glaring down at her with what looked to her more like fury than mere impatience. It was all she could do not to lower her eyes and back down the steps, mumbling an obsequious apology.

But—hang on. What was she supposed to be apologising for? She hadn't even asked for Mr Watson yet!

Late? *Late?* Well, whoever it was who was an hour late and responsible for inflaming his towering temper, it certainly wasn't she! Even if she was just about to make his temper a thousand times worse!

She smiled, uncertainly. 'Actually I'm not. Late, I mean. Although whoever you thought I was obviously is. I mean, I'm not her, am I?'

'You,' Marshall said, in a far from conciliatory voice.

'Well, yes, it's definitely me. Candy Harper, remember?'

'Only too well.' Marshall Scott scowled. 'Oh for heaven's sake, you haven't come to haul your damn children on to my terrace, have you?'

'My children? The terrace? Oh, I see what you mean. Fancy you remembering that! No, I haven't, actually, though it really is a very good idea. Perhaps some other time...if you didn't mind...'

'Then what on earth do you want?'

'I want Mr Watson, actually. Jack Watson.'

Candy's voice trailed away. Marshall Scott's stare had become so very, very intense by now that it was a wonder it wasn't burning a hole in her. Anger and incredulity seemed to be fighting to gain the upper hand in him. The overall effect was devastating—and devastatingly unnerving. She lowered her gaze and inched backwards to the very edge of the staircase.

'Jack Watson doesn't live here.'

'I do know that! But he was here on Sunday, and I thought... I assumed... well, he didn't come to my cottage again this morning, so I reckoned he must have come here instead.'

'Then you reckoned wrong.'

'Oh.' Candy tried to inch even further back, but there was a parapet in the way. 'Look,' she said, 'I'm awfully sorry. Really I am. I was so sure he must be here. I didn't think——'

'Obviously not,' Marshall interrupted her, as if to imply that it was evident she never did think about *anything*.

'I've said I'm sorry!' Candy retorted. 'It's all right, I won't keep you any longer!' She turned sharply away from him, and positively dashed down the stairs and back to her car.

'Another burst pipe?' Marshall's sarcastic voice enquired, just as she reached the car.

'Of course not! I don't flood out my kitchen every day! But I do need to find him urgently, because he's supposed to do some work for me, and I can't get on with anything else until he's done it.'

'Well, he's not here,' Marshall repeated.

'I do believe you!' Candy flung back at him.

'Wait a moment.'

Candy already had the car keys in her hand. She didn't want to stay a minute longer than she had to at Little Bixton Hall, even if there wasn't any reason to rush back to her Mr-Watson-less cottage. But politeness made her turn to see what Marshall wanted to say.

'Yes?'

Slowly, Marshall descended the stairs and approached her. He stopped a couple of paces away, and said brusquely, 'If you can't get on with whatever you were going to do, you can come and help me for a while.'

'Come and help you?' she repeated incredulously.

It seemed to dawn on Marshall that he hadn't put forward this suggestion in a way that would tempt her to accept it. Slowly his expression changed, from the scowl into—not exactly a smile, but a sort of grin, half-apologetic, half-amused.

'I'm held up too, because my model hasn't turned up for this morning's photo session. It's a rush job, so I can't afford to keep on waiting: I've got to get some photos out by tomorrow evening. I was just wondering if maybe you'd be willing to have a go at modelling for me. You're too short to make a fashion model, but you'd probably do for these shots. Your hair's all right, and the client wants back shots, so your face won't matter. It's not the ideal solution, but I think you'd pass muster. It's worth a try, at least.'

Modelling? Modelling! He was asking her to model for him! Who did he think he was joking?

'That's not funny,' Candy said in a tight voice.

'What's not funny?'

'Suggesting that.' She turned away from him, and fitted her car key into the lock.

She didn't get as far as turning it, though, because Marshall Scott's hand suddenly came down on hers, firmly, keeping it from moving at all.

'What makes you think I was trying to be funny?'

'I'm not quite that stupid, for heaven's sake! I can tell when somebody's trying to make fun of me, and I don't like it. So let me go, please.'

'I wasn't making fun of you, Candy. What on earth made you think I was?'

What made her think it? What a stupid question! Wasn't it obvious?

But it clearly wasn't obvious to Marshall, because he maintained his firm grip on her hand, and repeated his question when she didn't reply to him.

'Well,' she mumbled, not looking at him, 'it's obvious that I wouldn't do.'

'Not to me, it isn't,' Marshall retorted, prising her hand free and then pulling at it until she was dragged round to face him.

'But you just said so! You said I was too short, and——'

'No I didn't, Candy,' Marshall interrupted her. 'I said you were too short to make a fashion model, but I'm not asking you to model fashions. This is something quite different. I reckon you'll do for this. If I didn't think so, I wouldn't have asked you.'

'But I'm not photogenic at all. Honestly, I never have been. Everybody tells me so. And—well, it's not as if I look like a top model, do I?'

'So what do top models look like? Most of the ones I know look utterly different from each other. The only thing they have in common is the fact that they all have good figures, good hair and good skin. And so do you.'

That was true—or at least, not so obviously untrue that Candy could doubt whether he meant it seriously. She was slim-figured. Her hair wasn't elaborately styled, but it was in good condition, and her skin had always been clear. But that wasn't the same as being pretty, was it?

But he had said they would be back shots, hadn't he? Perhaps for this little job it really wouldn't matter that her face was never going to make her fortune.

'I'm not sure.'

'Please. Just as a favour, to make up for stealing Jack from me on Sunday, if you like! There's no one else I could ask. I've tried Caroline—Caroline Greenwood, that is—but she's working all day. I know I'll be taking your time up, but you'll get a fee, of course—quite a reasonable one if I find I can use the shots.'

A fee! Now that did make a difference. There was no disguising it, she really did need some extra money. She was uncomfortably aware by now that she had overestimated her do-it-yourself skills, or at least her strength, and that she would need to hire Mr Watson for longer than she had originally planned. Even a tiny fee would make a real difference to her skin-tight budget.

Could she? Could she really do it?

'Well . . .'

'Good girl,' Marshall said confidently.

'I haven't agreed yet! Anyway, what sort of photos are these going to be? I'm not taking my clothes off, not for anyone.'

'You won't have to, I promise. It's promotional work, for an advertising campaign. Very respectable.'

It didn't sound all that bad, she had to admit. It sounded rather glamorous, really. It was nice to have been asked to act as a model—even if they were going to be back views. But did she really want to spend her morning being photographed? Did she really want to spend her morning in the company of a bad-tempered Marshall Scott? Spending ten minutes in his company had proved unnerving enough, and even now she couldn't bring herself to meet his eyes.

But it couldn't be much worse than hanging around at Bell Cottage on her own waiting for Mr Watson finally to turn up, she thought to herself. She couldn't think of any hidden drawbacks. It would earn her that fee. And if she did prove a disaster and Marshall failed to get any shots he could use, she wouldn't have lost anything—certainly not Marshall's friendship or respect, because she clearly didn't possess a scrap of either!

'OK, I'll give it a try,' she said slowly.

'Right.' Marshall took a step backwards, releasing her at last, and narrowed his eyes in the cool, assessing look that seemed to be so typical of him. Candy flinched a little at the intensity of his inspection. She clinked her car keys nervously, and wondered what was going to happen next.

'You'll need a long dress,' he said. 'Nothing too bright or too fancy: something without sleeves, if you've got one. The detail won't matter, because it'll all be in soft focus. Can you manage that?'

'I've a navy-blue evening dress that might do.'

'Then go and get it. And you'd better bring some make-up with you, and a comb.'

'OK. I'll be back in half an hour.'

She opened the car door and climbed in, feeling awfully clumsy and un-model-like under his gaze. Marshall watched her in silence. Then he put his arm in the way just as she was about to close the door, leaned forward, and said in a low voice, 'Make it a quarter.'

What an extraordinary thing to happen! Candy could hardly stop laughing once it had sunk in. Modelling for Marshall Scott! Juliet would never believe a word of it.

But on reflection it really did beat waiting idly for Mr Watson, so she sobered down once she was back at Bell Cottage, and concentrated on getting together all the things she would need. A quick rummage through her wardrobe brought to light her one and only evening dress. Fortunately it sounded like the kind of thing he wanted her to wear. She held it up and gazed critically at it. It was navy-blue crêpe, low-cut, with little shoelace straps across the shoulders and a full, swirling skirt. More Top Shop than St Laurent, but it suited her, and that was the main thing.

She hauled her suitcase out from under the bed and folded the dress carefully into it, grabbed her make-up bag and added that, located a pair of evening pumps in case her feet were likely to be in shot, and finally, as ordered, threw in a comb.

That, and the journey between Little Bixton Hall and Bell Cottage, took considerably more than fifteen minutes, but it would do the ill-tempered Mr Scott no harm to wait, she thought to herself. It wasn't her fault that his real model hadn't turned up. Maybe he's terrible to work with, she thought. Maybe that temper scares models so much that they often chicken out at the last minute. But she had seen his temper already and survived it, so she reckoned she'd manage to live through another bout if she had to.

There had just been that moment, when he had first made the suggestion, when her sense of humour had deserted her completely. Andrew's brutal criticisms had made her supersensitive about comments on her looks, so Marshall had—unintentionally, she reminded herself—hit her on a very raw spot. But she didn't generally let the knowledge that she was no beauty keep her from enjoying life, and if Marshall really thought she could do it, then why shouldn't he be proved right?

Tact certainly wasn't one of Marshall's attributes, she thought ruefully. So she was too short, was she, and it was just as well that they would be back shots, so her face 'wouldn't matter'? *And* he'd only asked her because his beloved Caroline wasn't available! No wonder she hadn't exactly glowed with pleasure at his suggestion.

But surely he won't be crass enough to criticise my appearance any more? she thought to herself. And if he does say anything that threatens to upset me, I'll just have to remember how absurd the whole situation is, and do my best to laugh it off.

By the time she had shut off her car engine, the front door of the hall was open and Marshall Scott was standing at the top of the front steps.

He came down them while she was extracting herself and her suitcase from the little car, and reached out to take the case from her.

'Whereabouts do we go?' she asked.

'There's a dressing-room you can use to get ready. For the shots themselves, I want you out in the grounds.'

'What are they for?'

'It's an advert for a brand of bubble bath.'

Candy let out a snort of laughter. Glancing sideways, she saw Marshall frown, and she did her best to straighten her face. It might help her to treat this as a big joke, she thought, but it wouldn't help to show him that she looked on it like that. To him it was serious work.

'In here,' he said brusquely, pushing open a door just off the main hall. 'I'll leave you to it. Knock on the door when you're ready.'

He set Candy's case down on a small table and went out again, closing the door behind him.

Candy looked around, curiously. It was a plainish small room, with cream walls and brown brocade curtains. The only furniture was the table on which Marshall had put her case, a chest of drawers with a large triple mirror on top, and a couple of upright chairs. The room was thoroughly nondescript, telling her next to nothing about Marshall and his tastes.

Marshall Scott, the famous photographer of bubble bath commercials, she thought to herself, smiling, as she unfastened the catches of her case. It still struck her as laughable. There was nothing wrong with bubble bath, it was rather glamorous really, but there was something hilarious about the contrast between this hard-nosed commercial assignment, and Juliet's reverent description of Marshall as 'our famous local photographer'.

She had thought of him turning out earnest black and white pictures of grimy walls or dour old men, and here he was, as commercial as they came, making a mint out of glossy adverts for toiletries.

Can you really become famous taking photographs for bubble bath commercials? she wondered, giggling, as she stripped off her skirt and top and shrugged on an underslip and her long dress. Or does he do some more artistic work as well? She was tempted to ask him, but she wasn't sure if he would be flattered by her interest, or annoyed by her curiosity.

With a little wriggle, she did up the zip at the back of her dress, and smoothed it down over her hips. It was several months since she had last worn it, but her weight hardly fluctuated at all, and it still fitted well. Maybe she was on the short side, but she was a neatly proportioned size eight, and if she was to be photographed out of doors she reckoned it might be difficult for people to judge her height at all.

She crossed to the mirror, and peered at her face. He had said it wouldn't be in shot, but then he'd told her to bring her make-up with her. Should she put some on? Better do. If nothing else, it would boost her confidence if she felt that she looked her best.

She unzipped her make-up bag and applied small quantities of lipstick, blusher, deep blue eyeshadow, eyeliner and mascara. She smiled at herself in the mirror. She looked all right. Not stunning, not the kind to turn men's heads away from beautiful blondes like Andrew's new girlfriend Georgina or Caroline Greenwood, but perfectly pleasant and ordinary.

Marshall had been waiting outside in the corridor. When she opened the door he was right on the other side, only inches away from her. Candy stepped back a pace instinctively to set a wider distance between them. Marshall seemed to be the centre of a magnetic forcefield, and she could feel herself start to crackle when he came too close.

He didn't speak, he just looked at her, silently and intently. Candy endured his stare, without moving, for a good half-minute. I do look all right, she told herself. There can't be anything wrong, it's only a minute since I checked in the mirror.

The suspense was killing. She grinned nervously, and did a rapid twirl that sent the skirts of her dress flying out around her. She cruised to a halt, her dress subsiding like a parachute, feeling suddenly elated. I'm a model! she thought. No dirty jeans and old shirts today. Today I'm looking gorgeous in my very best dress.

Still he said nothing.

'Well? Will I do?'

'The dress will. That's fine. But your hair isn't quite right, and your face isn't right at all.'

Somewhere inside Candy, a bubble seemed to burst. Curse him! No wonder his models couldn't face turning up if he treated them like this! She had already made it embarrassingly clear that she was touchy about her looks. Couldn't he have realised that she desperately needed a few words of praise to boost her self-confidence?

'You told me nobody would see my face.'

'That's not quite what I said. I said the client had asked for back views, but all the same I'll take a variety of shots from all angles. I told you I wanted you made-up.'

'I *am* made-up.'

Marshall reclaimed the pace she had put between them, and stared straight into her face from a bare twelve inches away. Candy steeled herself to keep still while she suffered his close-up examination. She had never, never felt more horribly self-conscious. It was like sitting for an exam which she knew in advance she was going to fail.

It's all right for you, Marshall Scott, she thought mutinously. I bet your girlfriends never ignore you and stare at a good-looking man across the room. I bet they never criticise your new clothes, your hair-style, the way you walk and talk and sit. I bet you've never in your whole life spent a year trying harder and harder to please a woman who's never satisfied, only to have her toss you aside and take up with someone as different from you as he could possibly be. That's a pity. If it had happened to you the way it happened to me, maybe you wouldn't be quite so rottenly critical and condescending to me! Now I'm going to feel plain and dumpy and unattractive whatever happens, and if I look miserable on your wretched photographs, you'll only have yourself to blame.

She glared at him, but he didn't seem to notice, didn't meet her eyes. He was still studying her face intently, inch by inch.

'All this'll have to come off,' he said thoughtfully. 'The blue of your eyeshadow's too bright. It ought to focus attention on your eyes, not draw attention away from them. And your blusher is too low. It needs to be here, at the very top of your cheekbones. You need to take it all off and start again.'

He reached out a long finger, and traced a very light line across Candy's cheek, where her blusher ought to have been. She blinked. He was so close, so unnervingly close, and his finger burned a little trail of awareness across her nerve-endings.

'I'll have another go.'

'And . . .it's hard to explain. I know how you ought to look, but it's not easy to put it into words. Look, sit down, and I'll do it for you.'

'You!'

'Why not? That way I'll get what I want, and it'll be faster than telling you what to do. We need to get outside as soon as we can. The sky's just right at the moment.'

He strode past her into the room, picked up one of the hard chairs, and set it down again in the direct line of a ray of sunlight that was coming through the open window. 'Clean that lot off,' he said curtly, 'and come and sit here.'

Nervously, Candy crossed to the mirror, found her cleanser and a pad of cotton wool, and began to cleanse her face. From the corner of her eye she could see Marshall picking up her make-up bag and rummaging through it. He brought out the lipsticks, the eyeshadows, the blusher, one by one, and held them up to the window with a critical frown on his face.

Candy went to sit on the chair. Marshall continued his inspection for a minute, then he swung round to confront her.

'Is this all you have?'

'Yes!' she snapped back. 'I'm not a real model, don't forget! I'm an infant teacher. Vanity isn't my thing. I don't plaster on eight different shades of eyeshadow every morning to impress a class of five-year-olds.'

'But—oh, never matter. I'll just have to do what I can with this lot.' He came closer, and closer still, until he was standing right over her. 'Shut your eyes,' he said, 'and put your head back a little.'

Candy obeyed him. She waited, edgily, for the touch of his fingers. They felt light and sure, as he traced a new line of blusher a little higher on her cheeks, and smoothed it in. She could hear the low rhythm of his breathing, and sometimes as he moved she felt the warmth of his breath skim her face.

Heaven knew what Marshall was doing to her face, but it felt delicious, sitting there in the sunlight and having him minister to her. If she closed her eyes she didn't have to think about his disapproving expression. Though he wasn't lavishing praise on her, he wasn't saying anything sarcastic either. She liked the deft, efficient touch of his fingers. There was nothing disapproving about them. She liked the faint minty, spicy smell that he gave off. She rather liked having his concentrated attention. Earlier she had felt nervous and crowded by him, but now, though he was even closer to her, it didn't feel too close. It just felt companionable.

He soon finished with her cheekbones, and moved on to her eyes. What he did with them she couldn't tell, but it seemed to take a long time and involve a great many different operations. Every time he withdrew a little and rummaged for something different, she lifted her lids and peered at him through her lashes.

He could be a model too, she thought, as she watched him. The lines of his face, his colouring, the way his hair grows, springing vigorously up from his forehead: it's all quite perfect. Even that look of short-tempered concentration fits the image. He'd be no fun to live with, I bet, but he's glorious to look at. He could advertise—not bubble-bath, but high quality men's suits, or an international airline, or a top brand of cognac. Does he ever photograph himself, or get a colleague to take photos of him? His would be a good face to photograph. It's classically handsome, but it's interesting as well.

The touches grew less frequent, the pauses between them longer. 'Open your eyes,' Marshall said.

Candy opened them, and found herself staring into his eyes, a bare six inches away from her own. She tried to bring herself to look away, but she just couldn't do it. His eyes seemed to hold her, to transfix her. They were a dark, dark brown, deep-set and long-lashed, with black, dilated pupils in which she felt she was drowning.

Marshall moved closer still. Her vision blurred. His lips just brushed against hers, slid past, then returned and claimed hers firmly and confidently.

She was too surprised to respond. And the soft pressure only lasted for a moment before he was drawing away, his manner oddly curt and distant, and he was saying, 'I'll just do your lipstick, and then we'll have to hope we get outside before the sky changes.'

'I'll do that,' Candy managed to say.

'No. I don't want you looking in the mirror, it'll only make you feel self-conscious. Trust me, I know what I want, and that's what I've got. It's not perfect, mind, but it'll do.'

Marshall's hand, light but determined, cupped Candy's elbow as he guided her down a corridor that led away from the hall and the front door. He walked fast, as if he was more impatient than ever to get going. Candy followed him in a daze. Everything seemed surreal to her. Especially the kiss. Of course it hadn't meant anything, but all the same it had put a lift into her step and a gleam into her eye. At last he had seemed to realise how dispiriting she had found his criticisms; at last he had treated her as an attractive woman, and, though she knew how superficial it was, she couldn't help feeling more self-confident as a result.

They turned from the corridor into a large, light sitting-room. She recognised it immediately as the room she had glimpsed when she had been waiting for Mr Watson in the garden-room.

'Excuse me for asking,' she said, 'but where's the dog?'

'Blitzen?'

'Look, I know it's silly to be scared of him, but I can't help it. I've always been afraid of dogs, ever since I was a baby. And if I don't know where he is I'll be thinking all the time that any minute he might come bounding up, and——'

'He won't. I've shut him up in his run,' Marshall said shortly.

'Good. Thank you.'

Marshall didn't reply. He thinks I'm being idiotic, Candy thought. Again. Silly, scatterbrained Candy Harper, that's the image he has of me. Gosh, I must be going round the bend, if my head swims after a quick kiss from a man who doesn't even like me! I was stupid to agree to this. I always look awful in photographs, and Marshall Scott knocks me so far off balance I'm never going to relax. It'll be a miracle if we get through the morning in one piece.

They went through the garden-room, and on to the terrace. It was a cloudy day, Candy realised, but the sun was shining from just below the rim of the clouds, bathing the garden in a strong, almost horizontal light. No wonder Marshall was restless and hurried, she thought. That light might be perfect for his pictures, but at any moment the clouds could come down over the sun and bring a swift end to the session.

'Go and stand over there,' Marshall dictated. 'At the very edge of the terrace. Put your hands on the balustrade and look outwards across the valley.'

'Like this?'

'More or less. Move your hands further apart and look upwards a little. That's better.'

Candy gazed at the sky. She was very conscious of Marshall behind her. What was he doing? When was he going to start taking his pictures? To take her mind off her nervousness, she said out loud, 'So I've just come out of my nice hot bath——'

'Don't be ridiculous.'

'Don't tell me I haven't yet got into it! I'd be all smelly and disgusting and——'

'Shut up!'

She shut up. She was terribly tempted to turn round, but she didn't dare. There were torrents of footsteps from behind her, some slow, some fast and impatient. In between each burst was a pause. Slowly the pauses grew longer. It was like waiting for a firing squad. Could she afford to relax until he had picked his angle? She let her shoulders droop a little, and was punished with a quick, terse command to straighten them.

'It's not quite right,' Marshall said eventually. 'Let's try you about two feet to the left.'

Candy obediently shuffled along the terrace.

'That's better. The backdrop's right now, but your skirt's all wrong, you've messed up the way it hangs. Let me . . .' She brought her head round, trying not to move her body, and caught a glimpse of Marshall's tall figure approaching. He bent down behind her and juggled the long blue folds. 'There, that should do. But your hair's still not absolutely right.'

A cool finger touched her scalp. She jumped.

'Turn your head towards me.'

She tried to keep still as he ran his fingers down through her hair, again and again. He bunched it in his hands, and scrunched the ends. It's work, Candy reminded herself sharply. Just work, that's all it is to him. With maybe a tiny touch of flirtation thrown in, but you mustn't take that seriously. Remember, he's got a beautiful blonde girlfriend. He's not interested in you as a woman, he's just doing his job thoroughly.

So you might as well do yours properly too. Flirt back a little, act feminine for once. He won't take it seriously either, but it'll help the session go more smoothly. She batted her lashes at him, and grinned.

'That's better,' he said. 'I like the look, I want you looking slightly mussed up. As if you've just . . .'

'Come out of my hot bath?'

'Use your imagination.'

Marshall smiled, a wide lazy smile of pure sensuousness. Candy couldn't help remembering that kiss. She didn't need to be told to use her imagination; it was already working overtime.

Was this really the morning she had meant to spend helping Mr Watson with the kitchen plumbing? Instead, here she was standing on the terrace of a beautiful country house, in an evening dress, with a stunningly handsome man focusing all his attention on her. This wasn't to be confused with real life, but boy, was it fun!

'That's fine,' Marshall said, in a voice which held a strange touch of gruffness. 'Now turn back to the valley. Shoulders right down. Wonderful. Hold it exactly like that.'

Candy froze. She could hear him stalking backwards towards the house.

'No, you're frozen, that won't do. Keep that pose, but relax.'

Candy tried. Then Marshall rearranged her arms, moved her a little, and she tried again. He told her to lift her face up, lower it, look to the right, the left, grip the balustrade with one hand or with two. It went on and on and on.

It would have gone on all morning, Candy reckoned, if the sun hadn't finally, disobligingly, disappeared behind the canopy of cloud.

'Damn!' Marshall exclaimed.

Candy abandoned her instructions, and turned to look at him.

'You must have a shot that'll do by now, surely?'

'I'd have liked a few more.' Marshall lifted his face and squinted at the place where the sun had disappeared. 'Still, we'll maybe get a little more sun in a few minutes. Let's take a break, and then try something else.'

Something else! All this, for one lousy advertising shot! Oh, well, Candy thought, if it had done nothing else the morning had certainly cured her of any thought that modelling was a desirable career.

She collapsed on to a wrought-iron chair, as Marshall disappeared into the house. She lifted her wrist to glance at her watch, but in vain: Marshall had ordered her to remove it ages before. It spoiled the line of her arm, he had said. Was it lunchtime? She had no idea.

It was. Marshall made that obvious when he reappeared with a tray in his hands.

'It's a working lunch, I'm afraid,' he said as he set it down on the wrought-iron table next to her chair. 'Nothing fancy.'

That was the literal truth, Candy discovered when she found out what the tray held: chicken sandwiches cut rather thickly from brown bread, a couple of late peaches, and a bottle of Perrier water.

'Are you the cook?'

'No, Mrs Dobson is. She's fine on plain food, but she won't touch anything exotic.'

Mrs Dobson was presumably the housekeeper, the woman in the apron who had opened the door to Candy that morning. Solid and reliable, I'll bet, Candy thought to herself, but no substitute for a wife. He would do better with a wife. A wife might even iron out some of those temper ridges. Caroline Greenwood? Yes, bear that in mind when you flirt with him, Candy: you already know he's Caroline's boyfriend, and not for you!

They ate the lunch quickly, and in almost complete—though not unfriendly—silence. Then at Marshall's insistence they made their way down from the main terrace across a couple of lower terraces, and into the less formal part of the garden. The sun was still behind clouds, but Candy could see that the cloud cover was thinning, and there seemed a good chance that it would come out again before too long.

'I want you against the trees,' Marshall dictated. 'Leaning against this one here, I think.'

Candy dutifully walked over to the tree and leaned.

'No, that's all wrong. Put your hands behind you and arch your body forwards slightly. That's right. Then I want your head slightly to one side—no, other side—and your eyes looking upwards.'

Candy considered these instructions.

'This reminds me of a painting,' she said. 'A Pre-Raphaelite painting. I might be one of Rossetti's heroines, or Burne-Jones's.'

'That's right. Think of that.'

She thought of it. 'It's not very original,' she complained, a moment later.

'It isn't supposed to be. It's what the client asked for.'

'A Rossetti heroine?'

'Not precisely that. It was me who asked for that.'

'So you'd thought of it too?'

'Of course I had,' Marshall said—rather absently, because he was busy adjusting his focus.

That throwaway comment annoyed Candy, and surprised her. She hadn't thought of Marshall Scott as somebody who knew about paintings. He was the prosaic man who didn't believe in the I Ching. He was a photographer, not an artist!

'Were you thinking of a painting for the terrace shots, too?'

'Uh-huh.'

'Which one?'

'One by a Scandinavian painter. You wouldn't know it.'

'I don't think I know any Scandinavian painters.'

'You should. They had a good school of naturalistic painting around the turn of the century. I've a small collection of pictures myself, including the one I was thinking of. I'll have to show them to you.'

'I'd like that.'

'Let me just get the distance right, then you can relax until the sun comes out.'

Marshall fixed his distance, and signalled to her to relax. Candy glanced up at the sky. The cloud was still there, and she could see it would be a few minutes, at the best, before he could take his pictures. She looked back across at him, and he met her look, and moved companionably closer, leaning against a tree near her own.

'Have you taken lots of photos here?'

'In the garden? No, not yet. I only moved in a few weeks ago.'

'So why did you choose to do these shots here?'

'Because it's an ideal location for them.' Marshall glanced around his lovely garden with a proprietorial air, and went on, 'It's one reason I chose the house, because I reckoned there were so many good locations in and around it.'

'So you do this kind of thing all the time?'

'What kind of thing? Bubble bath advertisements? Good heavens, no!'

'Advertisements generally, then?'

'Quite a few. I take just about any assignments that interest me.'

'So why did this one interest you?'

He shrugged. 'Partly because it pays well. Mainly because I wanted to take pictures like these in locations like these.'

That wasn't very forthcoming. Candy turned to him, meaning to ask some more questions, but she saw immediately that he wasn't paying attention to her any more. He was squinting up at the sky, presumably trying to judge how the clouds were moving.

Her question died on her lips, and for a moment she just watched him. The sheer beauty of him enthralled her. He looked vital and healthy and alive, but at the same time he had a sensitive face. He was a thoughtful type, not a hearty kind of man. He really did have it all. Including that foul temper, she thought more prosaically; but even then there was a gentler side of him, the side that had mussed her hair and gazed into her eyes, smiled at her—and kissed her.

Change the subject, Candy, she told herself sternly. It's no use your going all dewy-eyed over a man like Marshall Scott. She stared up at the sun, or, at least, at where the sun should have been. The cloud seemed to be thinning slightly, and she could just make out a faint round disc.

'It's coming,' she said.

'What is?' Marshall glanced at her, and for just a second she met his eyes.

'The sunshine, of course.'

'Oh. Oh, yes, so it is.' Marshall spoke vaguely. Then he straightened up, and became brisk and business-like. 'We'd better get ready. I'll take the pictures as soon as the sun's out.'

He reclaimed his camera, while Candy moved her arms back and gazed dutifully into the far distance again. She was beginning to get the hang of this, she thought complacently to herself. Modelling might be boring, but it certainly wasn't difficult.

'No, that's not right.'

She brought her eyes back, grumpily, to Marshall and his camera. 'What's wrong now?'

'Your expression. You look as if you're wondering if it's going to rain before your washing's dry. Put some romance into it.'

'Think of my boyfriend, you mean?'

'If it helps.'

'I haven't got one.'

'Think about your dinner, then.'

Candy grinned; then, with an effort, pushed the grin away. Chocolate ice-cream, she thought. No, that's not right. Steak tartare. Sole bonne femme. Oysters and champagne.

'Wonderful,' Marshall shouted. 'Hold it!'

She held it. Though she didn't dare to look at him, she could sense Marshall snapping away a few yards from her. The thought of Marshall himself came back into her head. Romance, he had said—put some romance into it. She imagined him striding across the grass to her, seizing her in his arms, and making mad, passionate love to her.

For a moment her knees felt positively weak at the thought. Then common sense prevailed, and she realised how hilarious it was. Passionate love! Marshall's attitude to her was a million miles away from that! A few more friendly conversations might succeed in persuading him that she wasn't the blundering halfwit he had originally taken her for, but there was a fat chance of his losing any sleep over her.

'Open your mouth just a fraction.'

Candy did, but it was no use: cold reality had crept in and, try as she might, she just couldn't make herself feel dreamy and romantic any more.

'You're not concentrating,' Marshall complained.

'I'm doing my best!'

'Well, your best's not . . . oh, curse it!'

What now? Candy glanced at him, and saw that he was looking at the sky. He was doing that because the gap in the clouds had filmed over again, and the sun had once more disappeared.

'Doesn't look too promising, does it?' she said sympathetically.

'Not at all. I doubt if we'll have any more sunshine this afternoon. Still, I might have something here that'll do. We'd better call it a day.'

'Suits me fine,' Candy agreed.

'Come on, let's get back to the house.'

He left her at the door to the dressing-room. Candy went in alone. She was just starting to unzip her dress when she noticed the mirror: and, curious, went across to see what she looked like.

Good heavens! It was her own face that looked back at her, but at the same time it wasn't. It might have been her beautiful twin sister, except that she didn't have a twin sister, beautiful or otherwise. It hardly seemed possible that it was really her.

Marshall hadn't piled a theatrically dramatic make-up on to her. Everything he had done was subtle, and without rubbing off a scrap she could have driven home, or gone into the Poacher's Pocket, or out on a date, without causing any raised eyebrows—except through admiration. But somehow the blend of shades he had rubbed into her cheeks and round her eyes had given a new depth and shapeliness to her face.

It was barely possible to believe that she was really looking at the same old ordinary, roundish face. It looked as if her skin had been stretched tighter over the underlying bones. There seemed a new fullness to the curve of her lips. And her eyes: her eyes were a revelation! They were the same boring grey eyes, but the subtle blend of grey and blue shadows seemed to give new emphasis to them, so that they positively leaped out of her face.

Good heavens! Candy thought. Did Marshall Scott see this in me? I've lived with my own face for twenty-three years, and I didn't know that I could look like this.

This didn't look at all like the dowdy girl whom Andrew had thrown over. The girl who looked back from the mirror was the sort of girl that anybody would look at twice. She was the sort of girl a man might dream about; the sort of girl a man—even a man like Marshall Scott—might fall in love with.

CHAPTER FOUR

JACK WATSON finally turned up at Bell Cottage two days later. He didn't mention his absence, Candy didn't dare to offend him by asking what else he had been doing, and soon his tools were spread across the floor, and he was hard at work fitting Candy's new sink.

At mid-morning the doorbell went again. Candy stumbled over the mess of pipes and appliances to answer it, and found herself confronting Mrs Kipling, the village school headmistress.

'I just came to check that you're——' Mrs Kipling took a very dubious look around Candy's building site '—settling in nicely.'

'I will be by the time term starts, Mrs Kipling,' Candy said cheerfully. 'I'd offer you a cup of coffee, but right now I don't have any water!'

'That's perfectly all right,' Mrs Kipling said primly. 'I suppose you're finding it a little—er—difficult to make your teaching preparations?'

Candy was, but she didn't dare to admit it. 'Not at all, Mrs Kipling. I've got lots of projects all ready to start the children on.' It was only half true, so she crossed her fingers behind her back and prayed that Mrs Kipling wouldn't ask her too many questions about them.

Mrs Kipling didn't. She sat down, edgily, on one of the packing cases that had to serve as chairs. 'You won't forget,' she said, 'that there's a pre-term meeting next Monday.'

'Of course not. It's already down in my diary.'

'And there was just one other thing. The village fête. It's a pleasure to see teachers joining in village activities, but I think I should mention that I heard one or two adverse comments about your—er—"fortune-telling".'

'Really?'

'I'm sure you see it as perfectly harmless, Miss Harper, but it's not the kind of thing the school governors like to encourage.'

'So next year you'd rather I helped out on the Tombola?'

'I'm so glad you understand.' Mrs Kipling rose to her feet, and brushed down her skirt disdainfully. 'I can see you're busy, so I won't keep you any longer.'

Candy kept up a chatty conversation about the fine weather as she saw Mrs Kipling to the door. But when it was shut behind the headmistress she put her knuckles to her temples and made a very ugly face.

Adverse comments, indeed! An afternoon's fun in aid of the village hall fund, and some sanctimonious idiot would have to go complaining to prissy Mrs Kipling about it! Now she seemed to be under a cloud before she had even begun her new job.

And worse, she knew just who had done it. Among the throng of cheerful fête-goers there had been only two people, to her knowledge, who had expressed their disapproval of her Chinese Oracle. One was Mrs Kipling herself, and the other was Marshall Scott.

How dared he? What business was it of his? To go and complain about her behind her back, when he had been so comparatively pleasant to her when she had modelled for him! She scowled again, then glanced at Mr Watson, phlegmatically beavering away, and tried to keep her annoyance to herself.

But the thought of Marshall Scott kept recurring all through the rest of that day. She hadn't heard from him since the morning she had spent modelling for him, and somehow this little incident crystallised in her mind a sensation of having been let down by him.

What had she expected, though? she asked herself. She had known all along that he was Caroline Greenwood's boyfriend, and it stood to reason that a man who already had Caroline wouldn't look seriously in her direction.

She knew Marshall hadn't done any more than flirt mildly with her to lighten their day together, and, though she assumed that he would contact her at some time to pay the promised fee, she didn't have any reason to expect him to phone or call round. Nor had she run into him in the village; but then, everybody said that he kept to himself, so that wasn't really surprising.

Soon her irritation at Marshall was buried by her pleasure in the way the cottage was coming on. By the end of that day the cupboards were all finished and a hob, cooker, sink and washing-machine were in place and working properly. Candy was able to set to work tiling the kitchen floor and decorating, and by midday on her last free day she could look around with pride. Her living-room was still furnished with packing cases, as she didn't have enough money yet to buy the sofa and chairs she had her eye on, but the room was decorated in the pretty pink and pale green scheme she had planned for the whole cottage, the floor was carpeted, her chintz curtains were hung at a clean window, and beyond the archway that gave on to the kitchen everything looked almost like an illustration from a perfect homes magazine.

She went shopping that afternoon, stocking up with food and buying a table lamp with a pink shade that matched the newly painted woodwork. She cooked a simple supper, then sat down with a sheaf of folders to plan out some more project work for her class.

At around eight o'clock the doorbell rang. Candy looked up in surprise. She still didn't have many unexpected callers. Would it be Juliet, come to wish her luck for her first day at work? Or Mrs Kipling again?

It was neither. She opened the door to find Marshall Scott standing there. He was casually dressed in brown trousers and a bright red shirt, and had a cardboard folder under his arm.

'Oh,' said Candy, her eyes travelling upwards and connecting alarmingly with his dark gaze. 'Do come in.'

'Jack told me where you lived,' Marshall said. He slid past her and into the living-room. 'I tried to phone you, but I couldn't track down your number.'

'No wonder. There's a six-week waiting list for having new phones installed; I haven't got one yet.'

'That explains it.' Marshall looked around him, setting his hands on his hips in his habitual, deliberate pose, and narrowing his eyes. 'You've just moved in?'

'A month ago.'

'A bit rough, isn't it?'

'You should have seen it last week,' Candy retorted. Rough! she thought furiously. How dared he? My paintwork's gleaming, my carpet's immaculate, my curtains hang like a dream . . . I suppose my seating does leave a little to be desired, though.

'I'm glad I didn't.' He glanced at her, and seemed to take in her indignant expression. His voice softened as he went on, 'I like your colour scheme. Is it the same upstairs?'

'It's the same all over. It's only a little cottage.'

'That's good. Too many people make the mistake of chopping it up, trying something different in each room. I like consistency myself.'

'Do you?' Candy said, half appeased by his evident attempt to make up to her. So he did know the rules of giving compliments after all: to say something thoughtful and believable with conviction. But even so, to have called her lovely cottage rough! OK, Bell Cottage wasn't Little Bixton Hall, but it was the first house she had ever owned, and she didn't like to admit to herself that anything about it was less than perfect.

Marshall Scott himself was certainly less than perfect, she went on to herself; he might look stunning, but he acted like a bad-tempered billygoat. She had never yet caught him in a friendly mood for more than five minutes together, *and* there was the memory of that ungenerous complaint to Mrs Kipling, not to mention the uneasy prickling that she felt whenever he was around. He certainly wasn't the company she would have chosen to round off the last evening of the school holidays.

But he was at least a visitor of sorts, and her doorbell hadn't exactly been ringing all the time since she had moved into the cottage. So she remembered her manners, and said, 'Would you like some coffee? I've nothing stronger here, I'm afraid, but we could always nip down to the Poacher's Pocket if you fancy a proper drink.'

'Do you?'

'Not particularly. I start work tomorrow, so I was reckoning on an early night.'

'Then I'll have coffee, thanks. Black, no sugar.'

'Certainly, sir.'

Marshall followed her towards the kitchen, and he stood in the archway, watching her, as she filled the percolator and set it on the hob. Candy was embarrassingly conscious of him. She seemed to have fallen out of the way of entertaining unexpected visitors, and she wished the contents of her artwork project folders weren't spread all across the living-room carpet.

'The kitchen's new?'

'Yes. All new.'

'You've planned it well. Do you cook much?'

'Every evening, generally.' She turned down the gas as the percolator began to bubble, and looked over at him with a grin. 'Nothing fancy. I like good food, but it's not my idea of fun to dedicate my life to producing it.'

'Fair enough.' He paused. 'I brought the pictures.'

'Oh, the photographs.' Candy grinned again, to hide the sudden rush of embarrassment that seized her. She still found it unnerving to think of that glamorous stranger who had confronted her in the mirror at Little Bixton Hall. A couple of evenings earlier she had sat down and tried to reproduce Marshall's make-up for herself, and she understood now how he had achieved such a striking effect. But she didn't feel glamorous inside, somehow, and, though the girl in the mirror had been undeniably attractive, it hadn't seemed to be her.

Anyway, even if the front views in the photos looked like the glamorous stranger, the back views would still look like plain unadulterated Candy Harper. And Marshall was doubtless the type who would peer over her shoulder while she was looking at the photos, and point out every tiny imperfection in her poses.

'No need to quiver,' Marshall said brusquely. 'They're not bad. I've brought you a dozen or so of the prints, the better ones. I never show anyone the contact sheets.'

'Then let's see the prints.'

Marshall looked round at the living-room, as if he was appraising the packing cases and deciding once more that they wouldn't do, then he moved right into the kitchen. He delved into his cardboard folder, and pulled out a sheaf of coloured prints which he spread in a bright array right across Candy's immaculate new worktop.

Candy moved to his side, and bent over to look at them. It took only a brief glance for a tide of relief to swamp out her apprehension. These weren't anything like Juliet's or her father's happy snaps, which invariably caught her squinting into the sun with a strange expression on her face. They were excellent photographs, all of them.

The pictures were in soft focus, as Marshall had said he wanted them to be. Though they had been taken around midday there was nothing glaring about the light, and the colours were subdued, almost faded, adding to the romantic impression they gave.

Though she didn't normally like looking at herself in pictures, she certainly didn't have to wince at these. She looked reasonable in all of them, both back and front views. Quite possibly an expert would be able to tell that she wasn't a professional model, she thought, peering closely at a shot featuring an arm that seemed to be uncomfortably angled across her back. But on the whole, the poses into which Marshall had wrenched her looked both elegant and relaxed. She seemed unaware of the camera, lost in a romantic daydream. Chocolate ice-cream, she thought, as her eyes fixed on a close-up of her leaning against the tree, and she smiled silently to herself.

That was the best picture, she thought. There were a couple of shots taken on the terrace which were almost as good, but that was definitely her favourite.

She stole a cautious glance at Marshall. To her surprise, he wasn't looking at the pictures himself; he was looking at her, with an odd, disconcerting intentness. Their eyes connected, and a flash of physical awareness shot through Candy, almost as if he were touching her.

A split second afterwards the sensation was gone, and Marshall was smiling uncertainly as he said, 'You like them.'

'Yes—yes, I do. They're very good photographs, all of them.'

'I don't think they are absolutely my best. But they're all right; they're about what I expected.'

'Do the bubble bath people like them?'

'Yes, they do. They'll be using this shot, and this one.' Marshall reached out, and picked up two of the photographs he had taken on the terrace. He handed them to Candy, one in each hand.

She took them, and for politeness' sake she looked again, though she had identified the shots instantly. They were both good pictures, but they weren't the ones she would have chosen. For a moment she was disappointed.

'I prefer this one, with me under the tree.'

'So do I, actually, but all the same it's a good choice. The people at the ad agency know what sells. It's their job to produce the most effective advert, not to pick the most artistic photograph. Often they'll choose a shot that's a little unbalanced, for instance, so they can superimpose their copy on it. And these are the ones that look most like the picture I'd originally showed them, the Scandinavian one. I'll have to show it to you some time.'

'I'd like that,' Candy said absently. She half closed her eyes and looked again at the terrace pictures, trying to imagine how they would strike her if she flicked past them in a glossy magazine. They wouldn't have her leafing frantically back through the pages to take a second look, but then what advert did? They would certainly attract her passing attention, perhaps even a little admiration, if she were reading the copy opposite.

The scenery was lovely, and her dress looked fine. She certainly didn't have the coltish beauty of a Jerry Hall, but her figure looked slim rather than dumpy. Her hair was just slightly dishevelled where Marshall had run his fingers through it, with the sun shining through the loose strands. Her face didn't show at all. They were both back views. The Pre-Raphaelite-type portrait of her under the tree was a front view, but not the shots that the ad men had selected. Maybe that was why the tree picture had been rejected, why it wasn't what they had wanted.

She did look all right in the photos, though; she could see that she did. It's not that they didn't like my face, she told herself firmly; it's simply that they wanted back views all along. Marshall told you that, remember?

Enough preening. She swept the pictures swiftly together into a heap, and said lightly, 'Well, that's a relief. I really wasn't sure that I'd do all right as a model! But even if the bubble bath people are happy with them, I don't think I'll give up my day job just yet.'

'I shouldn't. It's a hellish life being a model. Oh, there's glamour of sorts, and good money for a lucky hard, boring grind for most of the girls who try it.'

'And I'm too short anyway,' Candy reminded him with a grin.

'True. But I'd like to take some more photos of you some time, if you'll let me. Not this kind of thing, but something more realistic. Without all the warpaint.'

'I don't look nearly as stunning without the warpaint.'

'No, but you look more real. More like yourself.'

More plain, Candy silently translated to herself. She was used to that kind of remark. It was the sort of comment that plain girls heard a lot. 'Don't worry, dear, looks aren't everything,' her mother had used to say. All right, they weren't, and no sane, intelligent person imagined for a moment that they were. But all the same, it was easier for the Marshall Scotts of this world to scorn physical beauty than it was for the Candy Harpers.

Look at you, Marshall Scott, she thought to herself. It doesn't take make-up and romantic settings and careful angling of the camera to make you look fantastic: you look as good as any film star I can think of, and all you're doing is leaning casually against my kitchen counter. It's a positive pleasure to look at somebody like you, while somebody like me gets accepted as part of the furniture—until a Georgina or a Caroline comes along, and then our men go chasing after them, and we're left to cry on our own.

She looked her best in the photographs, she knew—even better than she had known her best could be. But still she couldn't outshine a truly beautiful woman. It was flattering to think that Marshall Scott had turned his attention full on to her for a little while, but it would be folly to think that she might be able to distract him from Caroline Greenwood.

The stupid thing was that she was tempted to try. She couldn't help wondering how he would respond if she were to flirt with him again. Would he run his fingers through her hair once more? Would he kiss her again? Would he make love to her, if she made it clear that she wanted him to?

Would he *what*? Candy, Candy! she scolded herself. That isn't what you want. You know very well it isn't. It's no use thinking idly about the pleasure of loving him for an evening. Think on, think to the time when he says thank you and goodbye, and moves on to somebody taller and blonder and prettier than you. It nearly destroyed you when Andrew walked out on you. Imagine how you'd feel if you fell in love with Marshall, won him for a while, and then had to watch him too cast you aside.

Imagine how Caroline would feel, she went on inexorably to herself, if she knew what you were thinking right now. This is Caroline's man who's standing in your kitchen—the bad-tempered brute, in case you've forgotten!—and all you're going to do is enjoy looking at him. And you shouldn't even do too much of that, if it keeps on affecting you in such a very odd way.

To defuse the atmosphere, she said briskly, 'I'll think about that. Meanwhile, I'm planning to put my modelling fee towards a new sofa.'

'What a good idea. Do you actually sit on the packing cases, or...'

'I've been known to, when I'm wearing denims. I won't sit on them in a skirt: too much risk of splinters in unmentionable places! But really, I haven't had much time to sit down since I moved in. I've been working on the house until late most evenings. And when I do stop work, I usually just sprawl on the carpet for the half-hour or so before I go to bed.'

'That sounds wiser.' Marshall took a couple of long strides back into the living-room, and flung himself down on to the small area of carpet that wasn't covered in art materials.

In spite of her good resolutions, Candy's eyes followed every yard of his progress. He was a graceful man: he handled his long body with unfailing elegance, so that every move was a pleasure to behold.

'Shove that lot aside,' she said, as he reached towards one of the nearer pages of her coursework plans. 'I'll just pour the coffee, then I'll clear it away.'

She busied herself with the cups and the percolator, though all the time she could hear the faint rustle of paper behind her.

'You're an artist?' Marshall asked.

'Not really, but as an infant teacher I have to be a Jill of all trades. You need to be able to sing songs, tell stories, paint pictures, make models out of empty cornflake packets, even write computer programs, these days. Art was my major at college, though. I'd like to paint properly, but I haven't had the time since I started teaching.'

She picked up one cup in either hand, and made her way to where Marshall sprawled. He was running his hands through a little mountain of shredded paper.

'What do you do with this?' he asked, reaching out with one hand for the coffee-cup.

'Cloud pictures, I thought.' Candy claimed her own patch of carpet, a safe couple of feet away from Marshall's long body. 'It's packing material; I had a whole load of it stuffed around my china when I moved in. I thought I'd get the kids to make collages of the sky, blue sugar paper with yellow sticky-paper suns and big white fluffy clouds made out of this stuff.'

'Or sheep.'

'Or foaming bathwater. Clouds first, though. The children like to be told what to do for the first few weeks. When they're settled they'll be more willing to use their imaginations.'

'Mmm. Sounds like fun.'

'It is. Hard work, but fun. Like some music?'

'It depends what you've got.'

'Oh, I've quite an assortment. I like just about everything from Vivaldi to modern jazz-rock.' Candy put her cup down, crossed over to her stereo system, and fumbled through her records. 'This is my current favourite. Do tell me if you don't care for it: I can easily swap it for something else.' She brought the needle down on a record she had bought a few weeks earlier, quiet, jazzy pop music, and waited expectantly until Marshall's slight nod assured her that her choice fitted his taste as well as hers.

'Have you been a teacher for long?' he asked, as she settled back on the carpet and reached out for another sip of coffee.

'A year, full time, though I had quite a bit of practice while I was training too. I joined a big school in north London, near my college, then my sister Juliet told me a few months ago that a vacancy was coming up here, and I thought I'd try country life for a change.'

'A change?'

'I've always lived in London before. What about you? Have you been in Little Bixton for long?'

'Oh, I've been here all my life. I went away to college, of course, and very little of my work is local, so there have been months at a stretch when I haven't been near the place. But this has always been my home.'

'I hadn't realised you were a native.' Candy was genuinely surprised. She had had an impression of Marshall as a classic outsider: the newcomer to the big house, staying aloof from the local peasants. But a moment's thought reminded her that Juliet had spoken of him as if he had lived locally for years, and that he called Mr Watson 'Jack'. He must have moved to the Hall from a different house in the village.

'Oh, yes, born and bred.'

'Then your family must live here too.'

'Not any more.'

There was a bleak tone to Marshall's voice which brought Candy swinging round to look at him curiously. He didn't meet her eyes.

'It was a car crash,' he said in a harsh voice. 'When I was in my final year at college. Dad slid on some black ice and hit a tractor, coming down Smugglers' Row.'

'How awful.'

'It was quick, at least. He and Mum were both dead before the ambulance got there. A policeman came to my digs and told me. It was the day before I was due to come home for Christmas. That was the worst Christmas of my life.'

He hesitated only to take breath, then went on, in a sudden rush, 'I thought I'd go, then. Turn my back on the place and never come back. I never did like it here as a kid, I always wished I lived in London where everything seemed to happen. I put the house up for sale, but there weren't any takers; houses moved slowly in those days. Then I graduated and started to travel and work all over the place, and I stopped thinking about moving. Nearly a year later I had an offer for the house, and I was just amazed. What do I want to sell it for? I thought. It's my home.'

'So you stayed.'

'That's right. The place suits me, in a way. People keep to themselves round here, they don't push and pry as they do in some places. Even after it happened they kept their distance. The college staff in London, my landlady, my girlfriend, they all fussed over me till it nearly drove me mad. But the people down here knew I just wanted to be left alone.'

'I think everybody needs sympathy,' Candy said gently, 'when something dreadful like that happens.'

'I didn't. And I don't now.' He said this fiercely, almost belligerently, as if he was heading off the possibility of her showing him any pity.

Candy didn't dare to press him further. She changed the subject quickly. 'You haven't been at the Hall for long, I heard.'

'Oh, hardly any time. I only moved in a couple of months ago. I'd had my eye on it for years, of course. I was practically waiting for the Major to die so I could have it. I've had the money to buy a big house for years, but I never had the time or the inclination to look elsewhere for one, and my parents' house suited me all right until the Hall finally came up.'

'So where was your parents' house?'

'Three doors down from this.'

Candy started in sheer astonishment. One of the cottages! She had taken it for granted that Marshall's family were rich, but if they had lived in the cottages they couldn't have been. They must have been old Mrs Fry's neighbours, living just over the road from the Watsons.

It would hardly have been tactful to show her surprise, so she said in as level a voice as she could manage, 'I didn't notice it on the market when I was looking.'

'It wasn't. Mrs Greenwood knew a couple who were looking for a cottage in the village, so I made a private sale to them without advertising it at all.'

'That was lucky. For you, not for me.'

'I got a good price. This was a better bargain, even though you have had to do so much to it.' He named the price his own cottage had fetched. It was true, Candy realised. And not only had she got more of a bargain: she simply wouldn't have been able to afford Marshall's cottage, even if she or Juliet had heard that it was for sale. She said this, and Marshall nodded.

They sat in silence then, listening to the record. Candy's mind was full of what she had just learned. She didn't dare to say any more until she had absorbed it all, and adjusted the picture of Marshall she had already built up. Somehow she had imagined that his life had always been easy and effortless, but how wrong she had been! He hadn't been born to the grand manner, but to a very ordinary lifestyle, made extraordinary only by that terrible tragedy. Perhaps it wasn't a sense of superiority that made him so aloof, so much as a naturally reserved temperament that had been driven further into itself when his parents were killed.

A part of her wanted to ask more questions, lots of questions. But she sensed that he would resist if she seemed to pressurise him at all, and she didn't want to fall into the trap of making any more easy, false assumptions about his character. And though she was curious, she didn't feel any urge to talk for social reasons: she felt quite at ease staying silent.

It was just growing dark outside. Candy hadn't closed the curtains. She turned over on to her stomach, and looked out of the window. She could see the red sunset staining the sky over the roofs of the cottages opposite.

How peaceful it was. Marshall seemed peaceful too. He wasn't coiled up like a spring, as he so often seemed to be. It was more as if telling her that much had taken a weight off his mind, and relaxed him.

She cautiously twisted her head and looked at him. He was sprawled across her new green carpet, on his back, with his legs crooked and his hands laced behind his head. He was looking up at the ceiling. One foot tapped slowly, in time to the restful music.

It was so good to have somebody else's company, even if the somebody else was staring at the ceiling and not talking. Candy tried to remember when somebody had last called round at the cottage in the evening, but she couldn't recall anyone coming at all. Juliet invariably visited in the daytime before Patrick was in bed, and so did her other occasional visitors.

You're the very first person to come here in the evening, Marshall Scott, she thought. Should she tell him that? No: it might sound as if she was making more of his unexpected visit than he had intended.

Slowly, Marshall turned his head towards her. His dark eyes sought out hers, and fixed her in a long, steady gaze.

This wasn't the flash of awareness that Candy had felt earlier; this was a positive flood of it, surging through her body and making her conscious of every inch. She was suddenly intensely aware of the feel of her clothes against her skin, the rough texture of the carpet underneath her, the two feet or so of air that separated her from Marshall. It was as if she had been empty before, and now had suddenly been filled with a strange new essence. A magnetic essence, for it brought with it a physical pull: she ached to close that two-foot gap.

But she didn't move, and finally it was he who levered himself to a sitting position, and reached over to draw her closer to him. His arms enfolded her as he pulled her body gently against the long length of his.

How odd. She felt quivery and intense, and yet she had a sensation of peace and comfort at the same time. He seemed both the easiest and the most thrilling of companions. The touch and feel and smell of his body were so familiar, so utterly right that it might almost have been an extension of hers, and yet it was alien, intensely masculine, blindly arousing.

His mouth softly claimed hers, and his arms tightened, squeezing her against him. Her breasts seemed to come alive and her nipples were hard buds of awareness. His tongue thrust and explored in the soft damp cavern of her mouth, and little flames of desire flickered down her insides. Yes, yes! her heart thumped, and her hands clutched hungrily at his shoulders.

Marshall moved, covering her with his body, sliding his knees either side of hers, bracing himself with hands on the floor so that she had to arch and cling to keep the contact between their bodies. His lips roamed downwards, finding and nuzzling the little hollow at the base of her neck.

Candy let out a little groan of sheer pleasure. Marshall eased himself down till his weight was heavy on her and reclaimed her mouth. He kissed her for a long time, the urgency easing and deepening into a throbbing intensity of desire.

The record ended, and the needle started to click around the last groove. Candy barely noticed, she was totally absorbed in the delight of feeling, touching, tasting Marshall. But through her haze of longing she sensed his withdrawal, at first barely noticeable, as if it was not his body, but something inside him that was pulling away, then steadily growing until he had drawn completely apart from her and was looking down at where she lay on the floor.

Candy's breath was still coming in short pants. Her whole body seemed to be hot and alive and aching for him. But he had retreated completely now. He wouldn't even meet her eyes.

'I ought to be going,' he said shortly. He reached for his cup, and drained the last of his half-cold coffee. He got to his feet. 'Mustn't keep you from your fluffy clouds. Thanks for the coffee.'

'That's all right,' Candy said awkwardly. Her own euphoria was fast fading, to be replaced by a feeling of sheer embarrassment. What on earth had she been doing, kissing Caroline's boyfriend with such passion? It was absolutely disgraceful of her, and all the more so when it had clearly been no more than a momentary impulse of Marshall's, that had gone as quickly as it had come.

She pulled at the hem of her jumper, though it hadn't ridden up very far. She felt flushed and disarranged, but Marshall looked perfectly cool.

'I hope the teaching goes well.'

'Thanks. Hey, don't forget the photos.'

To her surprise he smiled, a proper warm smile that touched his eyes and lit up his face. 'I haven't forgotten them,' he said softly. 'Those ones are for you.'

* * *

Marshall's interruption meant that Candy didn't have as much work prepared to show Mrs Kipling as she had intended, but all the teachers at the village school were friendly and welcoming, and she left their pre-term discussion looking forward to starting work in earnest. Then the term began, twenty-seven four- and five-year-olds clamoured for her attention every day, and there was no time to think of anything but teaching.

She had thought life in the country was lived at a slower pace than in London, but that certainly didn't apply to the children, she thought ruefully, as she collapsed on to her carpet, exhausted, soon after three-thirty every afternoon. It was all she could do to find the energy to cook supper and prepare the work for the following day.

A month after term had begun, Juliet called round at the cottage after school one day and said, 'You're coming to supper on Friday, Candy.'

'I am?'

'No, you haven't forgotten.' Juliet smiled at Candy's guilty look. 'But we'd been saying, Peter and I, that you don't seem to get out enough at the moment. We haven't done much to introduce you to people locally, so we thought we'd have a go at remedying that. We've fixed up a dinner party for Friday, and you're to come.' She paused, and frowned. 'You're not going to be busy on Friday, I hope?'

'I wasn't before you invited me,' Candy responded cheerfully. 'But now I will be!'

'Put on your best dress for it.'

'Best dress?' A suspicion came over Candy. 'A man?'

'Well—yes.'

'Oh, Juliet!'

'Look, Candy,' Juliet said briskly. 'I know you're still moping over Andrew, but you've got to get over it, really you have. It's time you had a new boyfriend.'

'I'm not moping over Andrew!'

'Then show a bit more enthusiasm!'

'I am enthusiastic, honestly I am,' Candy said in a brighter voice. It was true, in a sense: Juliet was such a good cook, and she always looked forward to her sister's special dinners. 'And I'll dress up in my very best, I promise.'

Juliet frowned again, as if she wasn't entirely convinced by this display of eagerness. But she confined herself to making sure that Candy wrote the date and time down on her calendar, and bustled off to bath little Patrick.

I am looking forward to it, I am, Candy repeated to herself as she sat in front of her dressing-table mirror, dutifully reproducing Marshall Scott's style of make-up, slightly adapted to go with her maroon and blue striped dress. Juliet's right, it is time I looked for a new boyfriend. It's no good spending my time hankering after a man I can't have. All the same, thank heavens Juliet doesn't know that the man I find myself thinking about when I wake up at two a.m. isn't Andrew, but Marshall Scott.

To think about Marshall so much seemed idiotic even to her. She hadn't seen or heard from him since he had called around at the cottage. She kept reminding herself of his commitment to Caroline, but still it hurt that he hadn't contacted her in any way. She must have misunderstood the scene that evening, she had tried to tell herself; while her own attraction had been intense, perhaps he had simply been flirting again. But it hadn't felt like flirting at the time, and she wasn't really persuaded by her own argument.

However much he had been attracted, though, it clearly hadn't been sufficient to cause him to find her a place in his life, and she didn't have any option but to carry on doing her best to get over her disturbingly intense feelings about him. Maybe the man Juliet had invited would help her to do that.

She felt ridiculously nervous about the coming dinner. She wasn't used to this sort of staged situation. In London she had always met lots of people casually through friends and workmates and friends of friends, but that just didn't seem to happen in Little Bixton. In Little Bixton these things obviously needed stage-managing, and it was lucky for her that Juliet was there to organise it.

I do hope we get on, she thought uneasily. If we don't, Juliet will probably feel obliged to arrange another dinner party, and another, and another! I'm in no frame of mind to fall wildly in love with anyone new, but perhaps we'll hit it off enough to justify seeing more of each other. Juliet would be so pleased if that happened. And so would I, because it doesn't do anything for my self-confidence when Juliet looks on me as practically on the shelf, just because I'm older now than she was when she married Peter.

Candy was the first person to arrive for the dinner, but Peter had hardly had time to pour her a dry sherry before the next guests came. They were George and Mary Greenwood, Caroline's parents: Mary, an older version of Caroline, a tall, elegant blonde, and her husband, a pleasant, slightly ruffled-looking farmer. Candy had met them both briefly before, and they immediately passed on an invitation from Caroline to supper the following week.

Then the doorbell rang again. Peter disappeared to answer it, and reappeared a moment later with a man who greeted the Greenwoods like old friends.

'Candy, this is Paul Morland,' Peter said at the first opportunity. 'Paul, meet . . .'

'Candida, isn't it?' Paul Morland held out a hand. Candy took it, and found her own caught in a very firm grasp.

'Heavens,' she said, 'nobody's used my full name in years.'

'You ought to encourage them to. It's too pretty to shorten. Or would you rather be called Candy?'

'Gin, Paul?' Peter gently interrupted.

'Whisky, thanks, if you have some.'

Paul was a short man, only two or three inches taller than Candy herself. He had short brown hair, and an unremarkable face dominated by a pair of steel-rimmed spectacles and a large smile. He's somebody who knows absolutely everybody, I'll bet, Candy thought to herself.

'What do you do, Paul?'

'I'm assistant manager at a bank in Wansham.'

'Really? I ought to be opening an account in Wansham myself, I've been using a London bank up to now.'

'Then I'll have to persuade you to switch to us,' Paul said with a smile.

At the end of a delicious dinner Paul Morland offered to drive Candy home. She didn't feel any strong attraction towards the banker, but he seemed like an easygoing, likeable man, and she was already beginning to think that if he were to invite her out she might as well accept.

'Come into the bank one morning,' he suggested as he pulled to a halt outside Bell Cottage. 'I'll sign you up for one of our deposit accounts, and buy you lunch to celebrate afterwards.'

'Any chance of making it a Saturday?'

'Certainly, if that would suit you best. A week tomorrow? About a quarter to twelve?'

'I'll write it on my calendar before I go to bed.'

'Fine.' He bent over and unlatched the car door on Candy's side. 'Goodnight, Candida.'

'Goodnight.'

CHAPTER FIVE

'CANDY,' Caroline Greenwood said on the phone a couple of evenings afterwards, 'would you mind awfully if I changed our supper date from Wednesday to Thursday?'

'Not at all, if Thursday would suit you better.'

'It would. My boyfriend's back unexpectedly, you see, just on a flying visit for one day, and I do want to see him before he goes off again.'

'Of course you do.'

'Eight o'clock on Thursday, then. You know how to get to the farm?'

They quickly went through the directions, and rang off with the date fixed for Thursday.

The alteration wasn't inconvenient for Candy, and Caroline had been frank and apologetic about it, but all the same her Wednesday evening dragged. She spent it planning some work for her class, an occupation she normally enjoyed, but one rather too solitary to keep her mind convincingly off Marshall and Caroline.

The following evening Caroline met her on the doorstep of the Greenwoods' farm, and repeated her apology as they made their way indoors.

'It didn't put me out at all,' Candy insisted. 'Did you have a nice evening, Caroline?'

'Wonderful, thanks. We went up to London. We had a marvellous dinner at a French restaurant, and then we went dancing in a nightclub. My boyfriend's a super dancer. We hardly sat down, and I didn't get back home till four this morning!'

'Heavens, you must be tired by now,' Candy sympathised. It was understandable that she should feel just a little bit jealous, she told herself, when the highspot of her own social life was her planned lunch with the assistant bank manager.

She asked Caroline about Paul Morland. 'He's a really nice man,' Caroline assured her. 'Everybody likes Paul. I often run into him at parties, the cinema—he goes absolutely everywhere.'

'That's the impression I got.'

'I should think he's just your type.'

Yes, short and plain, Candy thought with a sourness that she couldn't altogether suppress, but that she hoped didn't show on the surface. She sensed that Caroline didn't mean to be bitchy. It was just that the other girl was used to being the centre of attention, and seemed to have relegated her without thinking to a minor supporting role: dowdy friend to glamorous heroine.

'I hardly know Paul,' she said carefully.

'I do hope it works out for you. Paul has lots of casual girlfriends, but there hasn't been anyone special in his life for a year or two.'

'It's not always easy to find the right person.'

'How true. I can't get over how lucky I am, with absolutely the perfect man! We must make up a foursome one evening, Candy, so you can meet him.'

No, thank you, Candy thought silently. She couldn't imagine keeping her attention on Paul when Marshall was around. But Caroline had already implied that Marshall had left for a working trip, so it seemed safe enough to take that to be an empty suggestion, and to assure the other girl that she would love to do it some time.

Whatever Caroline imagined, Candy knew by the end of their lunch that she wasn't going to be the perfect woman for Paul Morland, nor he the perfect man for her. He was pleasant company, but the necessary spark just wasn't there. They got on well, though, found quite a few common interests, and parted with mutual assurances that they would meet up again soon.

Candy didn't take it for granted that those assurances would come to anything, but Paul called a few days later to invite her to a party that Saturday, the first day of the school half-term. She was happy to accept, and they agreed that she would pick up Paul and drive them both to the party.

It was the first big party she had been to since leaving London in the early summer, and she prepared for it carefully. She thought of wearing the blue dress that she had worn for Marshall's photos, but in the end she decided it might be too dressy, and settled for black crêpe trousers and a silky pink top, dressed up with gold jewellery.

Paul, when she collected him, was casually but neatly dressed in a dark brown shirt and trousers. The party was held in a large, rambling house on the outskirts of Wansham. The two of them arrived early, but already the rooms seemed incredibly crowded. They had to push their way through crammed corridors to locate their host and hostess.

Candy knew almost nobody at the party, but Paul seemed to know everyone, and he was an attentive partner, introducing her to couple after couple until her head whirled with the effort of keeping all the names and faces straight. Two or three people invited both her and Paul to other gatherings, and she began to feel that by Christmas her social life would have livened up considerably.

She was chatting to an accountant and his wife when Paul reappeared by her shoulder and tactfully drew her away from them. 'Caroline's here,' he said. 'Joe and Liza are pretty dull, and you've been talking to strangers all evening, so I thought you might like to track down somebody you already know.'

'Sure,' Candy agreed, following him as he nudged his way, with many smiles and throwaway asides, through the crowded room. She was genuinely happy to go and find Caroline. She had found the other girl pleasant company, and she thought Marshall would still be away on the long trip Caroline had mentioned, so there would be no danger of facing the two of them together.

But no sooner had she seen Caroline, in a circle of six or seven people at the far end of the hall corridor, than she saw Marshall standing next to her. In an immaculate dark suit and tie, and white shirt, he looked far smarter than most of the people there; smarter than Candy had yet seen him, and as unreasonably handsome as ever.

Caroline was looking attractive too, in a long, slinky dress in pale peach. Candy suddenly wished she had worn her blue dress after all.

She paused for a moment, willing the hammering inside her to fade away, and reminding herself firmly that Marshall was a near stranger whom she hadn't seen for weeks. Then he looked across in her direction.

Just for a second, their eyes connected. There was the same flash of electric awareness that Candy had felt the last time they had met. The month in between that meeting and this seemed to fall away, and she felt as if it was only seconds since she had been in his arms.

Then Marshall smiled, an impersonal welcoming smile, and the sharp end of the sensation was gone.

He doesn't remember it, Candy told herself. It meant nothing to him. How could it have? He wasn't interested in seeing you again; he's with Caroline, just as you knew he would be.

He must kiss lots of women casually the way he kissed you, she went on brutally to herself. He must have just the same effect on lots of women. Perhaps it's some kind of chemical reaction that we all get when we gaze at tall, dark, handsome men! It's rather like going down a Big Dipper: your stomach falls away in a feeling that some people find terrible, but lots manage to enjoy. I ought to enjoy it. I ought to have found it flattering that he's flirted with me a little, even if it doesn't mean anything to him.

He's like Caroline, so much more attractive than the rest of us that it's natural to him to bask in admiration he doesn't return. It can't be anything new to him to have a woman go weak at the sight of him. To him, you're just another ordinary girl who fancies him like all the rest.

But, even if she was like all the rest to him, he wasn't like all the rest to her. How much simpler life would be, she thought, if only it were Paul Morland who made her insides do double somersaults.

Caroline also glanced her way. 'Oh, Candy,' she said, 'how nice to see you here. Do you know Bill and Tracy? And Philip and June, and Marshall?'

'I've met Marshall,' Candy said, smiling vacantly at him, and then at the rest of the circle. 'Don't you remember, Caroline? It was you who talked him into letting me tell his fortune at the village fête.'

'Of course,' Caroline said. 'I remember now: I had to bully him into going into your tent! And when I asked him afterwards, would he say what you'd predicted? Not a word of it!'

'You tell us, Candy,' June said.

'Absolutely not,' Candy responded. She was conscious of Marshall's eyes on her, but she didn't look his way. She laughed—half at her own stupidity in being upset by his presence, half at the memory of the fortune-telling session—and went on in a cheerful voice, 'All the fortunes I tell are absolutely confidential.'

'Will you do mine? What do you do, read palms, or tell the Tarot?'

'I've tried the Tarot, but at the fête I used the I Ching, the Chinese Book of Changes. Sure, I'll do yours any time: fifty pence towards the Little Bixton Village Hall fund.'

'Inflation!' Caroline protested. 'It was only thirty pence when Marshall and I had it done. But it's worth every penny.'

'Was it? Marshall, was yours worth it?' June persisted 'Has it all come true?'

'Not yet,' Marshall said. 'I did it for a laugh, but I really don't approve of fortune-telling, as Caroline knows very well.'

And so do I, Candy thought to herself. Suddenly she remembered something else, something even less comfortable. Marshall hadn't stopped at disapproving. He had gone as far as criticising her to Mrs Kipling, and souring the start of her new job.

A little flame of anger stirred in her. Curse Marshall! He had made her feel a fool, and he was still making her feel a fool: for not looking cool and blonde and beautiful like Caroline, for telling those silly fortunes and annoying Mrs Kipling, for going weak at the knees whenever he turned that routine smile in her direction.

It always seemed to be the Candy Harpers of this world who got cast as the cheerful comics, she thought angrily. The Marshall Scotts never had to act the joker; they always effortlessly slid into the role of leading man.

'You don't just not approve, as I remember,' she found herself saying, in a sharp little voice. 'I recall that you violently disapproved of my fortune-telling.'

The attack surprised him. She saw that in the expression that just flickered across his face, and in the barely perceptible tightening of his muscles.

'That's true,' he said coldly. 'I do strongly disapprove.'

'Did she embarrass you, Marshall?' Paul asked.

'Not quite, but she tried hard.'

'No, I didn't,' Candy retorted. 'I didn't have to try hard. The Oracle itself embarrassed him. I'll bet its answer was the most apt it gave all afternoon, even though I couldn't get him to admit it!'

'You'll never get Marshall to admit he's wrong about anything,' Caroline said with a laugh.

Marshall turned to her, and frowned. He's annoyed, Candy thought. He didn't like her saying that. He doesn't enjoy this kind of conversation one bit. He's not invulnerable after all. It really does embarrass him to be teased, and he absolutely hates to be criticised in public. That thought pleased her. She wanted to see Marshall squirm a little.

But Paul Morland clearly didn't, because he stepped in, saying in a casual voice, 'I don't really approve either, to tell the truth. These things seem to be pure chance, as far as I can see. Half the time they get the right answer and the other half they couldn't be more wrong. But if you were embarrassed, Marshall, it really was your own fault. It's a high-risk occupation, having your fortune told by a beautiful woman.'

Caroline laughed again, and June joined in. Marshall's brows lowered over his eyes. Candy laughed too. They were getting under Marshall's skin, she could swear. Maybe Caroline and June didn't realise it, but she did. Paul's intervention hadn't changed that at all. Marshall was prickling. Good. Let him prickle.

Marshall's defences weren't quite that leaky, though. He smiled, blandly, the effort it took barely visible even to Candy's intent eye. 'It seems to be a high-risk occupation encountering Candy in any circumstances,' he said in a cool voice.

'What a rotten thing to say!' Her protest came out instinctively. Immediately afterwards she knew it had been a mistake. Marshall had said it to deflect the group's attention on to her, and she had played right into his hands.

'Is it?' June said curiously. 'Why, what else has happened when you two have met?'

'I didn't realise you'd met since then,' Caroline said.

'Only by chance,' Candy said hastily, praying that Paul would rescue her again. But Paul wasn't alive enough to the undercurrents between her and Marshall to do that, and it was Marshall himself who went on, his voice sardonic now, his self control completely regained,

'Actually we met again the very next day, after Candy had an accident with her plumbing.'

'And whose was the high risk that day? Mine, all mine!' Candy turned to Paul. 'Imagine it! I was in desperate straits after a pipe burst in my kitchen and

DETACH ALONG DOTTED LINE AND MAIL TODAY! – DETACH ALONG DOTTED LINE AND MAIL TODAY! – DETACH ALONG DOTTED LINE AND MAIL TODAY!

flooded everything including me, and when I went looking for help I was practically savaged by Marshall's great wolfhound!'

'Wolfhound, indeed! Blitzen's a German shepherd dog, as you know very well. And if you hadn't tried to steal Jack away from mending *my* burst pipe, he'd never have come near you!'

'Yours wasn't a burst pipe! It was only an overflowing tank. Jack told me so.'

'Only an overflowing tank! You've never had an overflowing tank, or you'd never say that! I had a river running down my stairs! Just because I didn't end up looking as if I'd been dragged through a hedge and then dumped in the river...'

'Did you, Candy?' Caroline intervened.

'I looked like a woman in distress,' Candy retorted. 'Which I was! And did Marshall show me a shred of sympathy? Not a hope!'

'Now that's not true! I did tell Jack to go and sort you out, even though it left me without water overnight. And I didn't get a word of thanks from you.'

'Sounds as if Candy was in no state to be grateful to anyone by then,' Paul said lightly. 'I'm astonished, Candy, really I am. There was I thinking you were a cool and collected schoolmistress, and you turn out to be a real Calamity Jane!'

'I'm not!' Candy yelped. 'Honestly I'm not! It's just Marshall. He puts a hex on me. Every time we meet something disastrous happens.'

'*Every* time?' Philip asked. 'From the sound of it you've only met twice, not counting tonight.'

'Well, there was the incident with the bubble bath...'

'Now that wasn't a——' Marshall began, but Candy wasn't going to let him off the hook again. She had him this time, she knew she did. She went on, determinedly,

'Talk of risk-running! All I did was come up to the Hall to look for Jack, and I ended up being dragged into a modelling session. All because Marshall's regular model had decided she couldn't face a moment more of his bad temper!'

'It wasn't that at all,' Marshall tried to complain, but nobody listened to him.

'Caroline,' June said, settling herself down on the stairs, 'you and I absolutely must hear this.'

Oh, you must, Candy thought. You shall hear every last shred of it. I'll make it as funny as I possibly can. Laugh at me if you want to, I don't mind. But I'll make sure, if it's the last thing I do, that you laugh at Marshall Scott too. Because he will mind. He'll mind like mad, I just know he will.

She smiled at the thought, leaned against the banisters, and shrugged her shoulders. 'It was because I was so filthy, you see,' she said sweetly. 'Marshall decided I was lowering the tone of Little Bixton, and he made it his mission to clean me up.'

'With bubble bath?' Paul asked incredulously.

'The very best brand.'

She gave just half a glance to Marshall, mainly to make sure that he wouldn't escape. He couldn't, she was delighted to see; Paul and Philip were standing between him and the open end of the hallway. He had to stand there and keep a polite smile on his face as she spun out the story for as long as she possibly could.

She put it all in, from his first angry tirade on opening the door of the Hall to the very last moment when the sun had gone in. How impossible Marshall had been to work with, how demanding he was, how many poses he had made her strike, how difficult he was to please.

June and Philip, Bill and Tracy laughed like mad. Caroline didn't, but Candy only half noticed that. She didn't feel guilty about Caroline. She wasn't hurting Caroline; the other girl was obviously securely fixed in Marshall's heart, and the story was nothing to make her jealous, particularly when she had been offered the assignment herself.

It was Marshall whom Candy watched. He was still hiding his reactions well, but he was angry, very angry. The skin around his lips had turned white, and he was squeezing them together in a tight line. His hand clenched as she got in her best taunts. His temper, his fussiness, his tactless comments about her shortness: she played them all for everything they were worth and more.

'Candy,' June said, when she finally came to a halt, 'that's incredible. Gosh, I wish I'd been there and seen it all. But Marshall, she must be exaggerating just a tiny bit?'

Marshall didn't look at her. 'I'm not going to apologise for taking my work seriously,' he said in a low voice.

'Marshall, it's funny, for heaven's sake,' Caroline said. Marshall didn't give any sign that he'd heard her. He knows he ought to laugh, Candy thought, but he can't. He just can't.

'So can we see these incredible photographs?' Paul asked.

'Sure,' Candy said gaily. 'They'll be appearing in magazines, in—I don't know, a month, Marshall? Six months?'

'They won't be appearing.'

'Won't be appearing! But you said——'

'That's changed now. The company have signed up a top New York model to head their campaigns, and they're having the adverts reshot to feature her.'

'So Candy won't appear in the adverts after all?' June asked.

'No. They decided that they didn't want her to appear. She's too short, and too dark. She doesn't have the image they want.'

'It's a pity I couldn't do it, Marshall,' Caroline said. 'I'm fairer and taller than Candy.'

And prettier too, Candy thought numbly. Like the top New York model.

He had got his revenge. Damn him, he'd got it ten times over. If he had ever really been discomfited by her attack, there was no sign of it now. It was she who was knocked down to rock-bottom, her fragile ego shattered once more. The others rapidly changed the subject, and she had a chance to stay silent for a minute until she had recovered her self-possession. Then Paul made an excuse for the two of them, and drew her off to talk to somebody else. She hadn't given herself away any more than Marshall had. She wasn't disgraced. But all her pleasure in the evening was gone.

CHAPTER SIX

CANDY slept heavily that night—and shortly. Her mental alarm clock woke her at seven-thirty, just as usual. She lay in bed for twenty minutes, trying to persuade herself that she needed some more sleep, trying to stop thinking about Marshall Scott. Then she decided that she wouldn't be able to sleep any more, so she got up, dressed in her painting clothes, grabbed a quick breakfast, and began to mix up some wallpaper paste ready for papering her spare bedroom.

She had pasted the first two strips when the doorbell rang.

It was Marshall. Candy let go of the door-handle, and took an uncertain two steps backwards. She did it mainly to get away from him, but he took it as an invitation to follow her indoors.

He wasn't on the rampage this time, though; he smiled, almost nervously, and she realised that he had come to mend relations, not to pick another fight.

'I came to say sorry,' he said abruptly. 'I hadn't meant to tell you about the photos like that.'

'That's all right.'

'No, it's not all right. I knew you were touchy about them, and it was mean of me to tell you in front of everybody. But really, it had nothing to do with the quality of the photos. You could see for yourself that they were fine. It's just that the advertising agency decided to take a different approach. It happens all the time.'

'All the time?'

'Absolutely. Every week. Every day, even.'

'All that effort just gets thrown away, and you say it happens every day?'

'In advertising, yes. It's something you get used to. But you weren't to know that.'

'No. No, I wasn't,' Candy said slowly.

Was it true? She didn't know. She wasn't a professional model, and she couldn't have been perfect for the adverts, however expertly Marshall took his photos. Perhaps the agency had been disappointed with them. But still, Marshall was trying to salve her hurt, and that was thoughtful of him.

She felt that she ought to apologise too. If Marshall had been malicious in telling her so bluntly and publicly about the photos being scrapped, it had been largely because she had been baiting him earlier. She had been mean to him, too—and he really didn't know any of the reasons that lay behind her edginess with him. But she couldn't think how to apologise without making it clear that she knew he had been affected by her criticism. Most likely he thought that he had hidden his feelings better than that, and she hadn't noticed.

'It was a bit vicious of me to go on about your temper,' she said cautiously.

'Yes, it was. I hadn't realised I'd been quite that impossible to work with, though now I can see I was pretty hard on you.'

'It was worth it to get such good pictures. At least, I thought it was at the time, though it is a disappointment to think that they're not going to be used.'

'I'll keep them anyway, and maybe show some of them at a gallery some time.'

'Maybe.' He won't, Candy thought. They aren't the right kind of photographs for him to show in an exhibition; they're too obviously commercial. But she appreciated the kindness behind his words, so she didn't say this.

'Am I interrupting something?' he asked.

'I'm wallpapering my spare bedroom.'

'I'd never have guessed.'

At least he said this with unmistakable irony. Then you do realise that I don't always look like a plumber's mate on a bad day, Candy thought to herself. I suppose that's some consolation for being reminded that I'll never pass as a fashion model either. It was a reassuring sign, too, that they were back to their earlier spiky relationship. It hardly seemed believable now that they had kissed with such passion the last time they had been together in her living-room. It was obvious that Marshall couldn't really be attracted to her. She was too plain to appeal to a man like him, and they didn't even get on well with each other.

But she felt she had to make some sort of social effort now that he was standing inside her house, so she said with forced brightness, 'I would offer you some coffee, but my paper's all pasted and ready to hang, and I'm worried it'll stretch too much if I leave it any longer.'

'You'd better go and hang it, then. I'll make us coffee.'

Marshall, make coffee! That wasn't what she had expected at all. But she couldn't see how to refuse the offer. Anyway, if she did refuse it he would leave, and in a funny way she didn't want him to go just yet. 'Thanks,' she said. 'Mine's white with no sugar.'

She lingered for a moment, intending to show him where to find the percolator and the coffee, but

Marshall strode into her kitchen, seeming perfectly at home, and began to open cupboards with such aplomb that it was obvious he didn't need her help. So she made for the stairs, grabbed the first pasted strip, and began to hang it on the wall of her spare bedroom.

The first strip went on beautifully, but the second one proved to be a pig; there was a light-switch to be negotiated, and, however much she nudged and fiddled and smoothed, the paper just wouldn't hang straight. It seemed to take her forever. She couldn't help thinking about Marshall, nosing alone through her kitchen cupboards—which were quite tidy, fortunately—and waiting for the percolator to come to the boil. Would he venture upstairs when he had made the coffee? She reckoned he would; he wasn't the type to think twice whether he would be welcome in her spare bedroom.

Sure enough, he appeared in the doorway, with a mug in either hand, just as she was trimming the bottom of the strip.

'Pretty paper,' he said approvingly.

'Horrible stuff,' Candy responded. 'It cost me a fortune, and it's so thin that it tears if I even breathe on it!'

'Did you paste two strips at once? That was a mistake. With this kind of paper you shouldn't let the paste soak in at all. You ought to hang it right away.'

'If you're such an expert, you do it!'

'I'll give you a hand, if you like.'

He would what? Candy downed scissors, straightened up, and stared at him in astonishment.

He looked straight back at her, with a half-smile on his face. It looked as if he might really have meant it.

But for heaven's sake! There was she in her decorating shirt and old jeans, and there was Marshall in an elegant dove-grey sweater over a white shirt, and a pair of well-cut grey trousers. If those are decorating clothes, Candy thought prosaically, then I'm my Aunt Fanny. That sweater's cashmere, I'll bet; if he gets wallpaper paste on it, it'll be completely ruined.

Marshall noticed her pointed look, and glanced down at his elegant attire. 'You've got a point,' he said, as if she had spoken her thoughts out loud. 'I can't do it in these clothes. But my fishing gear's in the car; I could change into that.'

'You're serious?'

'Of course I am. I rather like wallpapering.' He put down the two coffee mugs on the end of Candy's wallpaper table, and gave her another smile—a wider one this time. Then he set off down the stairs again. He reappeared a moment later with an armful of clothes, and after checking briefly with Candy, who was busy cutting another strip of paper, he disappeared into her bedroom to change.

'I paste and you hang? Or vice versa?' his voice interrupted her as she was sloshing on a brushful of paste.

'I paste and you hang,' Candy said, glancing up appraisingly. Marshall's fishing gear consisted of an olive-green sweater with patched elbows and a pair of green corduroy trousers. It was almost as disreputable as her painting clothes, so for once she wasn't at a sartorial disadvantage. But it suited him, all the same. He looked like the sort of super-efficient decorator that you saw in television adverts for new brands of paint, all dark good looks and disgusting good humour as the paint and paper just fall immaculately on to the walls.

Good humour? Marshall? Candy did a double take. But she hadn't been mistaken; he was looking positively cheerful for once, as if he really did relish the prospect of getting to grips with her devilish wallpaper.

He certainly must like decorating, she thought; he can't have any other reason for wanting to help me with it! It can't be the pleasure of my company that he's looking forward to, even if we have buried the hatchet after last night's altercation.

'Suits me,' he said. 'Where's the plumb-line?'

Candy didn't possess one. Marshall was rather scathing about this, and about the fact that she hadn't removed the light switches and power sockets so that she could run the paper underneath them. His good temper didn't exactly disappear, but he seemed to manage to combine it with his usual dictatorial perfectionism.

Wallpapering with him was going to be exactly like posing for him, she realised with a sinking heart. He had probably enjoyed that too, curse him! He was the sort of man who got a real kick out of insisting that everyone around him lived up to his own sky-high standards.

But there was something rather pleasing about seeing a job organised efficiently and sensibly, and she could tell, even before Marshall started hanging his first strip of paper, that her bedroom was going to be decorated absolutely perfectly. Marshall might exasperate her by insisting on lots of changes from the rough-and-ready system that she had set up herself, but she had to admit that every one of them was for the better.

Once he had everything organised just as he wanted it he settled down to work with cool, efficient competence, and just the same good humour that he had shown earlier. Neither of them talked much, though Marshall whistled tunes half under his breath from time to time. They fell into an easy working rhythm, and almost before Candy knew it they had finished two walls and worked their way round the window.

'Don't forget your coffee,' Candy said. She reached for Marshall's half-empty mug, intending to hand it over, then hesitated, realising that it really was too cold to be drinkable.

'I won't.' Marshall reached out and took it from her, and downed the contents in a couple of large gulps. 'Years of practice,' he explained, handing the mug back. 'I always forget to finish my coffee, so I always end up drinking it cold.'

'You need someone to remind you.' The words came out automatically, then Candy bit her tongue, feeling that it hadn't sounded at all as she had meant it to sound. But Marshall made no comment, he simply picked up the strip of paper that was pasted and waiting for him.

'I'm sorry I was so touchy last night,' he said, as he guided the paper into perfect position.

Candy looked up from her pasting table in surprise. It was the last thing she had expected him to mention.

'You hate to be criticised, don't you?' she said curiously.

'I'm afraid I do.' Marshall gave her a wry smile. 'I know I ought to be more thick-skinned, but I'm not.'

'You hide it pretty well.'

'Not well enough.'

'Well enough for what?' Candy put her brush down, and stared at him.

'For people not to notice, of course!'

'I don't think anybody did notice except for me.'

Marshall didn't reply. He didn't resume his papering, but he didn't meet Candy's intent gaze either.

'Really,' Candy went on, 'I can't imagine that anyone in Little Bixton whispers about how thin-skinned Marshall Scott is. OK, you got annoyed when I made fun of you, but then *I* got annoyed when you made fun of me! Maybe people think you're a bit short-tempered—which you are—but I'm sure they're not laughing at you for being too touchy, Marshall.'

'It's easy for you to say that. You don't know——'

He stopped in mid-sentence. 'Know what?' Candy asked gently.

'Oh, never matter.' He picked up the scissors and turned away.

You *are* touchy, Candy thought to herself. That's true. I still don't think your friends deliberately tease you as a rule, but all the same you're usually quick to prickle when they do. Why? What is it that I don't know?

She didn't dare to ask him. They worked on for a few more minutes. Candy finished pasting her strip, and Marshall took it from her.

All the time she was thinking, about the incident the previous night and all that had provoked it. Finally she came to a decision. Marshall wasn't looking in her direction, he was busy at the wall. She watched him for a moment, working away, then said in as neutral a voice as she could manage, 'Do you actually know why I got at you last night?'

Marshall barely glanced up, then looked down again.

'I suppose because I—because I didn't . . .'

'Because you did! Because you complained to Mrs Kipling, you rotter!'

His eyes flew up to hers this time. There was blank astonishment on his face.

'Mrs Kipling? But I don't——'

'For heaven's sake, Marshall, it's no good pretending you don't know what I'm talking about. I know you did it.'

'Well, *I* don't know I did it,' Marshall said huffily. 'Did what? What on earth am I supposed to have complained to Mrs Kipling about?'

'About the fortune-telling, of course.'

Marshall frowned. 'Candy, you'd better explain right from the start, because I honestly haven't a clue what you're on about.'

'Oh, come on, Marshall! It wasn't exactly a secret that you didn't approve of my Chinese Oracle.'

'True, I didn't approve of it. I still don't. I think it's rubbish, and I've never hidden that. But why on earth should I complain to Mrs Kipling about it?'

'To stop me doing it again, I suppose.'

'Stop you? How could Mrs Kipling stop you? What's Mrs Kipling got to do with——' He stopped short again in mid-sentence, frowned, then said in a different tone, 'Oh.'

'Because she's my boss, remember,' Candy said in a deliberately patient voice.

'Now I do. But Candy—look, when am I supposed to have done this?'

'I don't know. At the fête, or just afterwards. Maybe after I came up to the Hall that first time. Back in the summer, anyway.'

'At the fête I didn't even know you were a teacher.'

'Then it must have been after——' Now it was Candy's turn to stop short. Belatedly, it struck her that Marshall wasn't reacting remotely as she had expected. She had expected him to strike back with a load of justification for complaining about her, but he wasn't doing that at all. Instead he was acting—well, acting as if he really hadn't known what she was talking about.

'But it must have been you,' she said uncertainly.

'Must it? Candy, who told you I'd complained? What exactly did they say?'

'Mrs Kipling did. She came round and said she'd had a complaint.'

'But she didn't mention me.'

'No, not in so many words. But then, I already knew that it was you who disapproved of my fortune-telling.'

'Well, someone else must have disapproved as well, because I certainly didn't say anything to Mrs Kipling. Heavens, I wouldn't do that!'

'Oh.' For a moment Candy was completely non-plussed. 'Then who did?' she said thoughtfully.

'I've no idea.' Marshall stood up, downed his scissors, and came across to her. He edged round the end of the pasting-table till he was next to her, and set his hands on her shoulders. 'Honestly, Candy, it wasn't me.'

Candy looked up at him. From his expression of concern, she felt sure he was telling the truth. It couldn't have been him. Whether he disapproved of the Chinese Oracle or not, he wouldn't have muddied her path with the headmistress. She could see now that that wouldn't have been his style at all.

'Then I didn't really have a reason for getting mad at you.'

'Certainly not that one.'

'A different one? What did you think it was?' What had he said? Because he hadn't—something?

'Oh, nothing important,' Marshall said in a not very convincing offhand voice. 'It doesn't matter now.'

Nothing seemed to matter right then—nothing except Marshall, who was standing unnervingly close, his hands still resting lightly on her shoulders, his dark eyes gazing downwards into hers. Candy stared back up into them, mesmerised.

She knew he was going to kiss her again. But there was a timeless instant, full of that knowledge, before Marshall's arms moved right round her, he pulled her up towards him as he bent down himself, and his mouth descended very firmly on hers.

It was like plugging in a thousand-watt light-bulb; it was like having a stream of warm honey poured into her veins. It was as blissful as the last time, and more so. A gently insistent tongue parted her lips, and moved between them to plunder the soft cavern of her mouth. Candy brought her own tongue into play, teasing and caressing and exploring as his was doing. Marshall pulled her body closer. She was on tiptoe, her arms stealing around his neck, her body fitting with surprising ease to the longer length of his.

Then he was lowering and loosing her, and she was unsteadily regaining her feet, and staring at him in amazement.

'I didn't mean that to happen,' Marshall said gruffly.

Candy's amazement rapidly gave way to a burst of sheer disgust with herself. Marshall hadn't meant it to happen? For heaven's sake, neither had she! Hadn't she told herself that she couldn't cope with this? Didn't she know that he was Caroline's man? Then what on earth did she think she was doing, encouraging him to kiss her in her back bedroom?

What on earth was she doing, responding to him in that frighteningly intense, unfettered way? Making herself look an idiot, that was what! Marshall Scott didn't really want her, as she was coming to want him. He couldn't.

'I think it's time for more coffee,' she said in an unsteady voice.

Marshall didn't reply, and as soon as her legs would obey her she made a half-rush for the door and the stairs, and the blessed solitude of the kitchen.

What was Caroline doing? Candy asked herself, as she emptied out the old coffee grounds and refilled the percolator. Where was Caroline, while she and Marshall had been wrapped in each other's arms in her spare room? Didn't Caroline and Marshall usually spend their Sundays together? From the way the other girl had spoken about her wonderful boyfriend, it hardly seemed conceivable that she would want to be apart from Marshall for a moment over the weekend.

There had to be a reason why Marshall had found himself on the loose. Perhaps Caroline was working. She had complained that her job as a businessman's PA often obliged her to work unusual hours, and they might include the occasional Sunday.

That had to be the explanation: that, or something very like it. Candy told herself this as firmly as she could. She had to keep reminding herself that she was a second-best attraction. If Caroline had been free, then obviously Marshall would have been with her at that very minute. As it was, he had only called around because he had felt he ought to apologise. It wasn't as if he had asked her out or anything.

Really he's a skunk, Candy, she went on to herself. You know how crazy Caroline is about him. You know he's seeing her and not you. It's crummy of him to kiss you when she's not around. No wonder he let go so quickly. He remembered her, and realised he was behaving badly.

Well, it won't happen again. You and Marshall are just two acquaintances, spending a Sunday morning together because nothing better's on offer. You'll be casual and friendly towards him, and he'll act just the same way towards you. That's how it's got to be. You keep it cool, very cool, or else you're going to get badly hurt.

When she carried two cups of freshly brewed coffee upstairs fifteen minutes later, the wallpaper looked to have crept quite a lot further around the bare walls of the bedroom.

'You really are very good at this,' she said approvingly, her eyes assessing the dead straight cuts at top and bottom of each strip, and the smooth expanse in between.

Marshall looked up at her. In a cheerful, ordinary voice that held no reminders of their kiss, he said, 'Of course I am. The amazing thing is that you're not so bad at it yourself.'

'Amazing! What's so amazing about that?'

'Well, you must admit, it's not exactly the image you put across. Look at the mess you got into with the plumbing . . .'

'I thought I coped pretty well with the burst pipe,' Candy retorted. 'At least I managed to find the stopcock myself and turn off the water.'

'And many women wouldn't have, I know. But at first, situations like that make people laugh. It's only afterwards that they look beyond the soaked jeans and think, heavens, she's fitting her own kitchen single-handed!'

'Almost single-handed.'

'Near enough single-handed,' Marshall said firmly. 'A little slip of a thing like you, all fluff and chaos on the surface, and you turn out to be the most competent woman I've ever met.'

Candy thought about this. 'I'm not the most competent woman *I've* ever met,' she said, challengingly. 'There are lots of women who are really good at do-it-yourself. You don't have a very high opinion of the female population, do you?'

Marshall groaned. 'You're not a women's libber as well!'

'Of course I am. Every sensible woman is.'

'Sensible woman! You mess around with Chinese Oracles and heaven knows what, and you call yourself a sensible woman!'

'That I do, I'll have you know.' Candy banged the coffee-cups down on the end of the wallpaper table to underline her point. Marshall straightened from where he'd been crouching by the skirting-board, and she thought for a minute that they were going to end up having another blazing argument, but he seemed to change his mind, and he simply moved forward to pick up his coffee.

'We ought to stop for lunch some time in the next hour,' he said consideringly. 'If we keep at it afterwards we'll have the room finished by mid-afternoon. Then perhaps you'd like to come back with me and see my Scandinavian paintings. If you hadn't planned anything else, that is.'

What a nice suggestion. It was tempting. In fact, it was more than tempting. Candy wanted to see the picture that had inspired the bubble bath photos; she was curious to see more of Little Bixton Hall; she wasn't looking forward to saying goodbye to Marshall and being left on her own. But it wouldn't be wise, she told herself. That certainly wouldn't rate as keeping things cool.

'I'd love to see them some time, Marshall,' she said. 'But not this afternoon, I'm afraid. I'd been planning to pack up at three and then go over to Juliet's—my sister's—for tea. She's having a couple of friends round, so I really can't get out of it.'

Marshall gave her a curious look, and Candy thought for a moment that he had seen through her rough-and-ready fib. But he simply said, 'That's a pity. We'll have to make it some other time.'

'We will,' Candy agreed. 'Now, where's the roll we were cutting? I'll just measure out the next strip.'

They had lunch together in Candy's kitchen: mounds of toasted sandwiches and fruit to follow. Marshall too seemed to be resolved to cool things down, and he showed the same easy but low-temperature friendliness towards her as she tried to show towards him.

They talked about their hosts at the party the day before, and about a few other mutual acquaintances in Little Bixton and Wansham, though they steered well clear of Caroline and of Paul Morland. Candy told Marshall about Juliet's family. Then, feeling a little guilty for having wrapped him up in her own concerns all morning, she tried asking him about his work, and to her surprise he responded enthusiastically.

He was about to start work, he told her, on the illustrations for a travel book set in Eastern France. He talked interestingly about the difficulties of getting pictures that satisfied his own artistic instincts, and also showed all the features that the writer wanted them to show. Candy knew enough about art and photography to ask some leading questions, and he opened out, talking at length as if he was glad to have a chance to air some of his preoccupations.

'It's funny,' Candy said, when Marshall came to a pause in his long explanations, 'but I never thought of photography before as a real art form.'

'I know,' Marshall said with a groan. 'You see us all as literal-minded realists trying to make up for the fact that we can't paint.'

'Literal-minded, certainly. Isn't that true?'

'Only in as far as it's true of most art. We try to show people the world, but we select and focus what we show them, so that with our help they see the world in a new way. Most painters do the same; writers too, in a way.'

'You love it, don't you?'

'Photography? Yes, I do. It's a job that's never boring, always challenging.'

'Never repetitive?'

'Oh, often repetitive.' Marshall gave her his sardonic smile. 'There are only so many ways of photographing a landscape, or a shot of a model for an advertisement, or a portrait. Almost all of them have been done before. Anyway, I don't always look for gimmickry. I try to create a style of my own, but most of all I just try to make my own pictures the best of their kind.'

'Which they are.'

'The best of them are, I think.' He pushed his empty plate aside, and stood up abruptly. 'Come on, let's get the rest of it over with.'

The rest of the wallpapering went very smoothly. However much they had argued in their earlier encounters, Marshall and Candy seemed to understand each other when they worked together. Candy was happy to admit that she was the less expert of the two of them, and to act as Marshall's assistant. He seemed to take that for granted—indeed, rather too much for granted!—but even so, she found a quiet satisfaction in anticipating when he'd ask for brush, scissors or pencil, and handing them over to him.

By two-thirty they were cleaning up in a perfectly decorated bedroom. He did that thoroughly too, and took on his share of the dirty jobs so naturally that it cost Candy an effort to realise that he was really doing far more for her than she had any right to expect.

'It's been so kind of you to help,' she said. 'I'd been expecting this job to take a couple of days out of my half-term holiday, and it's no fun working on your own.'

'Always goes faster with a bit of help,' Marshall said lightly. He paused, then went on, almost diffidently, 'You're on holiday next week? Does that mean you'll be free tomorrow?'

'Not tomorrow: I'm going on a day trip with another of the teachers and her family.'

'And Wednesday I'm leaving for France. How about Tuesday? Is there any chance you could come over and look at my paintings then?'

'I'd love to,' Candy said, before she had time to stop and remind herself that she ought to be saying no.

'Come in the afternoon, and stay for supper. I'll pick you up. About four o'clock?'

'OK,' Candy said. Her doubts were surfacing now, but she pushed them back. She had already said yes, and she couldn't get out of it without seeming rude.

Anyway, she wanted to see the paintings. It would just be a friendly encounter; it wouldn't really be dangerous.

'I'll see you then.'

He didn't make any move to leave, and it struck her that he had no fixed plans for the rest of the afternoon. It seemed a little ungracious not to suggest that he come with her to Juliet's. But she couldn't let him know that the tea-party had been a figment of her imagination; and anyway, she still wasn't confident that their truce was going to last.

'I won't invite you to Juliet's,' she said awkwardly, 'because it'll be a real hen party, all mums and toddlers! But I'll really look forward to Tuesday.'

'So will I. I'll just grab my clothes.'

'You'd better change.'

'No, I'll do that back at home.' He ducked into her bedroom, picked up the bundle he'd left on a chair, and almost before Candy could catch her breath he had deposited another swift kiss on her forehead, disappeared down the stairs, and was revving up his car—a rather flashy Porsche, Candy saw, peeping out of her bedroom window—outside in the village street.

Candy really did go round to Juliet's—though not to a proper tea-party—and was disconcerted to be greeted with a barrage of questions about Paul Morland. Her mind was so full of Marshall that she had almost forgotten she had spent the previous evening with Paul, and it took an effort to shift mental gears, and talk about the bank manager instead.

'You don't sound very thrilled about him,' Juliet complained.

'Don't I? I'm sorry, Juliet. I think I'm just tired from lack of sleep and too much decorating. Paul's good company, and I'm hoping to see him again before too long.'

'Good for you,' Juliet responded. 'So what's on the horizon, Candy? More parties? Candlelit dinners for two? Us staid married women rely upon our little sisters to provide some excitement at second hand!'

'You get plenty of that from Peter and Patrick,' Candy teased. She dredged her mind, and managed to recall three or four of the couples who had issued invitations to her and Paul at the party. Juliet was soon appeased, and when Candy tried to change the subject to Patrick's approaching birthday party, she didn't persist in asking more questions.

Candy didn't mention her invitation to Little Bixton Hall. She had told Juliet—in a jokey way—about her trips up to the Hall to look for Jack Watson, and about the modelling, but she hadn't made a big thing of her acquaintance with Marshall Scott, and this didn't seem the time to refer to how it was developing. Juliet knew her too well. However nonchalant she tried to sound, she suspected that Juliet would see beneath the surface to that frighteningly intense attraction she somehow couldn't manage to kill off.

She felt sure now that it wasn't wise of her to have accepted Marshall's invitation. But what else could she have done? It would have been rude to refuse. I mustn't let it lead to anything more, though, she told herself. Maybe I really should see as much as I can of Paul Morland; he might help to distract me from Marshall. Though Juliet perhaps imagined there was more to that than appeared on the surface, she was confident that Paul wouldn't misread her intentions.

She made herself a cup of coffee once she arrived home, only to decide when she had half drunk it that it had been a mistake. She felt more edgy and jumpy than ever. Her thoughts just wouldn't calm down.

After a while she went to her little desk, and took out the I Ching in its black cover, and the little bundle of sticks that she used with it to tell fortunes. Marshall might think the Oracle is rubbish, she thought to herself, but I don't. I can't talk to Juliet about him, but I feel I need some kind of feedback: maybe the I Ching will give me some.

She rummaged for a stick of incense, lit it, and waited until the strong sweet smell began to fill the small room. Then she spread out her piece of black silk, laid the book down on it, and bowed ceremoniously three times to the Oracle.

A question: that was the easy bit. Please, Oracle, tell me how to deal with Marshall Scott. She knelt down on the carpet with the sticks in her hand and began on the long, slow routine of shuffling and counting that would give her the pattern of a hexagram.

Slowly it took shape. Young Yang; Young Yang; Young Yin . . . She wrote down the six lines, one after the other on a scrap of paper, then took the book and searched her tables to find out which hexagram the Oracle had given her.

'Lu': 'Treading'. She knew that one, since it had several times caught her attention when she was looking through the book, though she had never turned it up before in a reading for herself. The Oracle's decision had all the familiarity of a favourite poem. He treads on the tail of a tiger, but it does not bite him. There will be progress and success.

He? Curse the Oracle, she thought to herself; it rarely allowed for women consulting it! 'He' was surely herself. And Marshall the tiger? She liked that. It rather suited him.

There was more. Nine in the fourth place: he treads on the tail of a tiger, but does it apprehensively and with great caution. In the end there will be good fortune. Then the hexagram transformed into a second one: *'Chung Fu'*, or 'Inmost Sincerity'.

At this, Candy couldn't help smiling. Inmost sincerity. Good fortune. Even pigs and fishes are moved by it... The superior man gives careful thought to criminal cases, and hesitates before invoking the death penalty.

What did it mean? Don't ask yourself that, she told herself. Let it sink into your unconscious mind. Listen to what the Oracle tells you. And above all, do what it tells you to do most clearly of all: take things gently!

CHAPTER SEVEN

CANDY spent a good half-hour on Tuesday puzzling over what she should wear to Marshall's. She wanted to look smart; for too many of their encounters, she seemed to have been dressed in her very scruffiest clothes! But at the same time she didn't want to overdo it.

She wasn't the type to boast a wardrobe full of sexy little black dresses, anyway; but after rifling through her two or three dinner-party dresses she came to the conclusion that none of them would do for a four o'clock visit to look at some pictures. Finally she settled on a brown outfit, a cord skirt and a lighter-coloured sweater with a pretty shawl collar, but even then she spent several minutes in front of the mirror, wondering if it wasn't perhaps a bit too understated.

But a little understatement was what her bizarre relationship with Marshall needed, she reminded herself firmly. If Caroline was there, and dressed in something infinitely more alluring, then that would just remind her of the stark realities of the situation.

Caroline wasn't there, though, nor anyone else either. Even Mrs Dobson the housekeeper had the afternoon off, as Marshall explained after she had hopped into the Porsche next to him.

'Mrs Dobson's left us supper,' he said, 'but she had to go and visit a friend in hospital in Wansham. So the house will be deserted.'

The tiger's lair indeed, Candy thought to herself. But there was no reason for her to be nervous about being alone with Marshall in his house when he had already spent most of a day alone with her in hers, so she didn't comment on the arrangement.

'It's a super car,' she said instead.

'The Porsche? Yes, isn't it?' Marshall smiled in a satisfied way. 'Some people have muttered that it's flashy for Little Bixton, but actually it's a very practical choice for someone like me. I usually travel alone, and I regularly go long distances, so I need something that'll eat up the miles.'

'Do you drive fast?'

'Oh, very!' He threw her a quick glance. 'Some people tell me it's over-compensation for my fear. But I just like it.'

Fear? The memory of the crash that had killed his parents suddenly came back to her, and a little shiver ran down her spine. What extraordinary mental defences Marshall must have, if he was able to confront the possibility of being afraid of driving, and still deny it to himself so thoroughly that he would choose one of the most powerful sports cars available.

There were depths to him that she hadn't yet begun to plumb, Candy thought to herself. Harder still to face was the fact that it wasn't open to her to explore them, that she felt she had no option but to try to keep her distance.

'I like it too,' she said edgily.

'Mind,' Marshall continued, 'I never break the speed limits. I couldn't afford to be banned from driving! But in the right situation this little beast will top a hundred with no trouble, and once or twice I've taken it higher than that.'

'Not up Whiskey Lane, I hope!'

'No, that would definitely be breaking the limit! I only go that fast on a proper track. I'll have to take you racing some time. But not today; that takes some planning.'

They scrunched to a halt on the gravel forecourt of the Hall, and a moment later Candy was following Marshall up the steps to the front door. She waited by his side as he worked through a succession of locks and flung the door open. A large furry shape came hurtling out of it, and Candy backed so rapidly that she nearly fell off the steps! She had taken the word 'deserted' literally, and hadn't realised that of course Blitzen would be loose in the house, acting as a guard dog while it was empty.

'Sorry about that,' Marshall said, slipping one hand around her waist to steady her, and extending the other one to Blitzen. 'I should have warned you about Blitzen's style of welcome.'

'That's what you call it!'

'He's only being friendly. See, he's not growling, he's just glad to see us.'

No, he wasn't growling, but he was straining forward from the collar that Marshall now had in a firm grasp, as if he wanted to know Candy considerably better than she wanted to know him. She took an edgy step away from both him and Marshall, and said nervously, 'Good dog.'

'Say it as if you mean it,' Marshall commanded her. 'And give him a stroke, for heavens' sake. Friend, Blitzen. This is Candy, she's a friend.'

Candy didn't feel like Blitzen's friend, but she obeyed as well as she could, and Marshall nodded his approval of her efforts. 'I'll shut him away in a moment,' he said, 'but he's been on his own for much of the day, and it's hardly fair to lock him up the moment I come home. Let's all go into the house.

He'll see it's all right then, and in a minute or two he'll settle down.'

To Candy's relief, the big dog did seem to settle once they were indoors: he flopped on to the flagstones of the hallway, panting gently, as Marshall read quickly through a note that Mrs Dobson had left for him.

'Anything important?'

'No,' he said, glancing across at her. 'Just instructions for when to switch on the oven and so on. Now would you like to see the pictures first and have a drink afterwards, or vice versa?'

'The pictures first, please,' Candy said.

'OK. They're upstairs. Do you mind if Blitzen stays with us? I'll lock him away if you're really scared.'

'I'll be all right as long as you're there too.'

'I promise not to leave you alone with him.' Marshall said it with a lightness that was only a step away from ridicule. He thought she was being idiotic, Candy knew. But she couldn't help it, the Alsatian really did frighten her, and though she was doing her best to act calmly she didn't like in the slightest the idea of confronting the dog without Marshall at hand to rescue her.

Marshall held Blitzen's collar as they made their way up the handsome curved staircase. Were the pictures in his bedroom? Candy wondered. It wasn't a bedroom that Marshall led her to, though, but an upstairs sitting-room, a long room with a series of tall windows looking out to the front of the house. It was furnished comfortably but rather shabbily, with a selection of battered sofas and chairs arrayed around an expanse of faded Chinese carpet.

'Not my style of décor,' he said, anticipating her reactions. 'I haven't been in the Hall long enough to get everything as I want it. This is some of the furniture I bought with the house. I want to get rid of it before long, and replace it with something more modern.'

'Not too modern,' Candy protested.

'What's too modern?' he teased. 'Spiky and uncomfortable, you mean? No, that's not my style either. I like furniture that's as comfortable to use as it is good to look at.'

'Big squashy sofas.'

'Maybe, or leather chesterfields; something that goes with the style of the house, and doesn't drown out the paintings.'

'Mmm.' Candy's eyes were still appraising the room. What elegant proportions it had! It would take very little effort to make a room like this look good: but with taste and money to direct its furnishing it would look absolutely superb. Lucky Marshall, to have a home like this to decorate! But he had earned it, she reminded herself; not long ago he had been living in a cottage similar to hers, and it was his own hard efforts that had brought him this beautiful house.

'This is the terrace picture,' he said, loosing Blitzen's collar and striding across to where a large painting hung between two of the tall windows.

Candy cast a nervous glance at the dog—who was placidly ignoring her now—and then followed him.

It *was* the terrace picture; she could see that immediately. The girl in the picture, staring out across a stone balustrade at a view of lakes and mountains, bore no visible resemblance to herself. She wore a long white dress and had her hair in a pigtail, hanging down her back. But the light, the pose, the atmosphere of dreamy thoughtfulness: Marshall had translated those perfectly from painting to photograph.

'Do you see the resemblance? It's always annoying; it was so clear in my mind, but now I look at the painting I almost wonder where I got the idea from.'

Candy tore her eyes from the canvas, and transferred them to Marshall. There seemed to be a hesitant note in his voice.

'Oh, yes, it's very clear.'

'She's nothing like you, I know. But there's something...'

'You've captured it wonderfully.'

A slow smile spread across Marshall's face; he seemed visibly to relax. He had been pushing for the reassurance, Candy realised; in a funny way, he had really needed her to reassure him that the resemblance was real. It struck her as odd. Marshall was a famous photographer, at the top of his profession, with a solid reputation behind him, and yet he didn't have the easy confidence in himself and his abilities that she might have expected from somebody in his position. He was aloof and defensive, and yet at the same time he had such a very evident need for praise and encouragement. It was a strange combination. Something in his past must have caused it—but she didn't think it could have been the car crash. The more she considered it, the more she felt sure about that. There was something further back in his life, perhaps in the pattern of his family relationships, which had made him the way he was.

Did Caroline know what it was? Did he talk to Caroline about the things that troubled him? Did Caroline give him all the love and reassurance he craved? And if she did, then why did he seem to need them from her, Candy?

That was a dangerous line of thought. She broke it off abruptly and said, 'Who painted it?'

'A man called Richard Bergh, a Swedish painter. He's one of my favourite artists. And this one here's by another one, a Norwegian painter, Harald Sohlberg...' Marshall turned away and strode off down the long room. Candy stood watching his long strides for a moment, then she followed him.

There were half a dozen paintings in the room, most of them smaller than the terrace picture that Marshall had led her to first, but all of them similar in date and style. Candy liked them all at first sight, but she liked them even better after listening to Marshall tell her everything he could about the scenes and the artists who had painted them.

It seemed that her initial burst of enthusiasm had been enough to break down his reserve; he was eager, even boyish in his manner now.

'You really love these pictures, don't you?' she said gently, when he made one of his rare pauses for breath.

'Yes, I do. Love is the only word for it. I first saw pictures like this perhaps fifteen years ago, on a trip to Norway, and ever since I've been building up my own collection. It's not just having the money to buy them; it's waiting for the right pictures to come up for sale, tracking them down... it's been a sort of obsession of mine.' He turned from the picture in front of them, and smiled almost apologetically at Candy.

'It's a very nice obsession to have,' she said.

'And an affordable one, thank goodness. Lovely pictures like these don't come cheap, but they are within my budget. Now, if I had a passion for Rembrandt, say...'

'You'd have to slave away for a lifetime just to afford one tiny sketch,' she finished for him, laughing.

'Longer than that, I should think! I do well as a photographer, but not quite *that* well! Now I promised you a drink, didn't I . . . ?'

They made their way to the downstairs sitting-room, where Marshall poured two gin and tonics, saw Blitzen settled on the hearthrug, handed Candy one glass, and raised the other to her.

'To . . .'

'Perfect wallpapering,' Candy said, cutting short the pause as Marshall considered what to say.

'Wallpapering it is. I'm not sure it was absolutely perfect, but we did make a pretty good job of it. I don't suppose you'd care for a job as a decorator here?'

'I certainly owe you a day's help in return for yours,' she said, smiling. 'If you could fit it in this week, I'd gladly give it to you.'

'I can't, I'm afraid, unless you want to do it alone.'

'You're off to France.'

'That's right, early tomorrow morning.' He gave her a slow smile. 'And to tell the truth, I've booked a firm of professional decorators to do the Hall from top to bottom early next year, when all the plumbing and wiring has been checked over and put to rights.'

'That's sensible. It really would be too much for you to do yourself, even if I did give you some help!'

'It would, I know. But I've always decorated my own houses, and it still seems strange to call on somebody else to do the work for me.'

Candy didn't reply. She was still struggling to make sense of Marshall. It wasn't that he was inconsistent, she thought to herself. The reserved, almost arrogant man who bit people's heads off, and the man full of unexpected enthusiasms and flashes of dry humour, were recognisably one and the same. It was almost as if he had a public face and a private face. But she didn't think it was really anything to do with his being lord of the manor; he would have been just the same, she reckoned, when he had lived next to old Mrs Fry.

'Actually,' he said, breaking into her private thoughts, 'there's one point on which I really could use your help. I can't decide how to decorate a couple of the spare bedrooms. I like your taste in furnishings; would you mind having a look at them, and telling me if you've any ideas that I could use?'

'That's real flattery.' She smiled, to show him she was teasing. 'And I thought you were only being polite when you admired my choice of wallpaper! I'd love to, Marshall. I've so many ideas, and only space enough in the cottage to try out a very few of them.'

'Want to take a look now?'

'Yes, why not?'

He rose to his feet, setting his glass down on a side table. 'Come on, then,' he said. 'I'll give you a tour of my country mansion.'

'Would you like to see all of the house?' Marshall asked, as they made their way back to the front hall. 'Or would that be too much of a good thing?'

'Oh, all, please.'

'There are no antiques, no heirlooms, I'm afraid.'

'It's a beautiful building, though. It would be worth seeing even if it were completely empty.'

'Much of it is,' Marshall said with a quick sideways smile.

He showed her the downstairs first. There was a huge formal dining-room, a second sitting-room that he called—half-jokingly—his morning-room, a study lined with books, and the little dressing-room she had used when she had modelled for him. They paused in the kitchen, which was vast, but to Candy's eyes appallingly primitive in its fittings, and Marshall switched on the oven to heat up Mrs Dobson's chicken casserole. Then, laughing, they went down a rickety wooden staircase to the cellar, full of cobwebs and brick pillars and dark corners that Marshall's torch barely lit.

'Will you take photographs here?' Candy asked.

'Oh, yes! In fact I've done some already—I'll have to show you. I want to clean up this side, install electric light and use it as a wine cellar, but the other side I plan to leave just as it is, fading whitewash, cobwebby alcoves and all.'

'What fun,' Candy teased. It *was* fun, creeping around in the gloom, but when they emerged she couldn't help shaking her head vigorously to make sure that no spiders were lurking in her hair!

They drifted through a long series of sculleries, dairies and tiny rooms that seemed to have no conceivable function; then Marshall led them to a back staircase, and up to the upper floor.

There was less to see here, because he didn't show Candy the suite of rooms that Mrs Dobson used, and he barely opened the door of his own bedroom before guiding her past it. But Candy was coming to have an impression of the house, and she could easily tell the rooms full of the furniture he had bought with the Hall from those he had already refurnished in his own style. His rooms were emptier, with just a few beautifully crafted pieces of modern furniture, and a great many pictures and photographs on the walls.

'I'll show you the attics—that is, if you'd like to see them—and then we'll finish up in the bedrooms I mentioned,' Marshall said, as they paused at the foot of yet another staircase.

'I would like to. Are there windows? Do they have a view?'

'There's a tremendous one from the back attic. That's my workroom. Mind, it might be a little dark to see it properly by now.'

He led the way up, and opened the door at the head of the stairs. 'This way,' he announced. He strode down a long dark corridor, and threw open a second door.

By the time Candy reached it, he had already gone through into the room. She paused in the doorway, staring in amazement at what lay beyond.

Where the rest of the Hall was solidly traditional, and slightly shabby, this was all hi-tech perfection. The floor was varnished and polished till it shone like mirror glass; the walls were painted a blinding white; the huge space was sparsely filled with the stark lines of floodlights, movable screens, and a huge angled desk set under the middle one of the three dormer windows.

Marshall stood in the centre of his domain, under the harsh light of a dozen powerful bare bulbs, with his hands set on his hips in an arrogant gesture of ownership. 'Well?' he challenged.

'It *is* too dark to see the view.' She knew it wasn't the praise she might have given, but she was taken aback by the room. She wasn't ready to praise it yet, and she didn't expect Marshall to feel the need for instant compliments.

But perhaps he did need them, because the strong line of his shoulders drooped almost imperceptibly. Then he straightened up and said briskly, 'I don't think it is, quite. Wait a moment.'

He strode towards where Candy stood at the door, and flicked a dozen lightswitches. One by one, the powerful lights went out. The two of them were left standing in the dusk of a late autumn afternoon.

'Come right over to the windows,' Marshall commanded. He took Candy's hand and pulled gently at it. She followed him across the polished floorboards.

'Now.'

She hadn't closed her eyes, but he said it as if he expected her to open them, and the effect was precisely as if she had. The view was vast. It spread in rolling waves of hill and valley, field and woodland and hamlet, for what seemed like miles and miles, until it faded into a dusky smudge on a far, far horizon. The sun was setting, and a sky of red and orange and yellow and grey streaks crowned the whole glorious scene.

'Isn't that something?'

Candy's face spread into a broad smile of sheer pleasure at the beauty of it all. 'It's just about everything,' she said in a whisper.

'Not quite everything,' Marshall said. 'There's this, too.'

She turned to him, wondering what he was talking about; and then the expression in his eyes told her.

His kiss this time seemed as carefully judged as the house, the room, everything around them. His mouth just brushed hers, then withdrew; then came back, more confidently; then withdrew again, only to return with the firm certainty that was already familiar to her. He gathered her to him carefully, giving her time to bring her arms around his shoulders and to settle her body against his.

I didn't mean this to happen, Candy thought faintly, but she was powerless to stop it. The pleasure of touching him, of tasting and smelling and seeing him, was so intense that she simply couldn't have resisted it.

'You know I'm falling in love with you,' Marshall murmured, his mouth barely a fraction lifted from hers.

'You can't be.'

'I'm no good at all this, I know. But give me time.'

On the contrary, he seemed to be very good at it. His hands drifted downwards, cupping Candy's buttocks and effortlessly taking her weight. His lips strayed, depositing a path of little kisses down the side of her neck and nestling in the hollow of her collarbone. He pulled her jumper free of her waistband and slipped a cool hand underneath to cup the straining curve of her breast. In a daze, Candy felt herself responding, the tip hardening in pleasure at the expert light touch of his fingertips, the flesh swelling in anticipation and longing.

'Marshall,' she whispered. This wasn't sensible, it barely seemed real, but it seemed as if he could resist it no better than she could herself.

The harsh ring of a telephone, only inches from where they stood, broke abruptly into their idyll.

'Damn,' Marshall said, raising his head and meeting her eyes. 'I'd better answer that—might be work.'

Candy couldn't make her voice function. She didn't move, didn't protest as Marshall gently disengaged himself, moved a step sideways to where the phone stood on top of a filing cabinet next to his desk, and picked up the receiver.

It *was* a business call, she sensed that almost immediately from the harsh, competent bark of his voice. His body seemed to tense; at one point he tapped his fingers on the surface of the desk, impatiently, as he waited for the other man to finish speaking.

It was as if she was forgotten. All the warmth he had shown a moment before had been switched off as abruptly and totally as the lights had been earlier. He was once again the short-tempered stranger who had treated her so aggressively when they met.

And heavens, what had she been doing? She had made a million good resolutions to treat him impersonally, just as she ought to treat Caroline's boy-friend, and all of them had melted like ice-cubes in front of a roaring fire the very minute he had touched her. As usual.

What on earth was Marshall up to? Telling her he was falling in love? That was plain ludicrous of him, as ludicrous as his pretending that he wasn't experienced at all this kind of thing, when she knew perfectly well that that couldn't be true. Wasn't his relationship with Caroline proof that he regularly went out with stunning women?

She fumbled to tuck back her sweater, and ran her fingers through her mussed-up hair to straighten it out as best she could.

Marshall had turned his back to her; he seemed totally absorbed in the telephone conversation. He reached for a pad of paper and a Biro, made a couple of notes, then pulled out a chair from under the desk, sat, and made a lot more notes.

She wandered across the room, trying to distract herself from him and to retrieve her composure. The kiss shouldn't have happened. She mustn't let things go any further. But curse him, why was he acting like this? He seemed to have forgotten the entire incident already. Maybe he too was thinking of Caroline.

Maybe this remoteness was his way of handling the guilt he must feel.

She walked to the door, and slowly and deliberately flicked on each of the light switches, one after another, until the whole room was bathed in bright, efficient, unromantic light, and the glorious view was no more than a faint sketch, overpowered by the reflections from within the room.

Marshall glanced round at her, mouthed an apology, and gestured towards the phone and his paper, to indicate that he would be some time. He didn't look guilty, damn him, just apologetic and distracted.

Candy drifted again. There were no photographs or pictures on the wall of this room: it was all purely functional. But she saw a big map chest against the far wall, and went over to this. Tentatively—glancing back at Marshall, who nodded encouragement—she opened one of the drawers.

This was obviously his work: heaps of it, sheaves of prints all neatly labelled and divided by sheets of tissue paper. She withdrew a big sheaf, and began to leaf carefully through the photographs.

They weren't romantic soft-focus shots like the ones he had done for the bubble bath advert; these were black and white photographs, with lines as hard and elegant as those of the room itself. The first batch were all views of an unfamiliar industrial town; the second that Candy drew out were portraits of a well-known actress, the third were studies of coal-miners.

'That's all my last year's work,' Marshall said, putting down the telephone receiver, crossing over and standing next to her. He rested an arm lightly across her shoulders, and his hand caressed the soft fall of her hair. He shouldn't do that, she thought. She ought to feel angry and tense when he behaved like that. But she just felt confused. Somehow, she didn't seem to be able to read the signals he was sending out.

'I'm very organised,' he went on. 'There's a drawer per year for my archives, and a separate filing system, all cross-referenced and indexed, for the negatives.'

'There must be thousands of pictures here.'

'There are: thousands of full-size prints, and hundreds of thousands of negatives. I never throw anything away. Mind, I used to find it difficult in the cottage; they took up the whole of my back bedroom.'

'I can imagine.' Candy glanced at the huge chest. She couldn't imagine how it would conceivably fit into a modest-sized spare room like hers.

'I'm not stopping you from looking,' Marshall said, moving his hand from her hair and putting it on the prints as if he was planning to do just that. 'But there's too much to take in at once, even if you weren't already suffering from sightseer's overkill, and we really ought to go down and check how our supper's coming along.'

Mrs Dobson's supper turned out to be excellent: fresh cream of onion soup, followed by the casserole, which by then was meltingly tender, and with cheese and fruit to finish. Marshall poured wine, and put on a record of chamber music so that the huge dining-room wouldn't seem quite so gloomily empty.

Candy was careful to drink only one tiny glassful of wine, in spite of Marshall's gentle insistence that she have more; she was determined not to get carried away again, and she worked hard to keep the conversation to impersonal topics. Marshall seemed to sense the change in her mood, and he didn't touch her again, or press her in any way.

It wasn't the most relaxed of meals, because she had to make a conscious effort to be as wary of him as she felt she ought to be. But even so, they seemed to have plenty to say to each other. Marshall told her long tales of the village when he had been a small boy, when Mrs Watson had been the local beauty, donkeys had been tethered on the village green, and the Poacher's Pocket had been carpeted in sawdust.

'How odd,' Candy mused. 'It wasn't all that long ago, and yet the world seems to have changed almost beyond recognition.'

'Village life has changed, I think, far more than town life. In those days everyone in Little Bixton knew each other. Today that's simply not so, and it's not just that I've changed myself.'

'That's true,' Candy agreed. 'Half of the children in my class have parents who commute to London to work. Little Bixton isn't a self-contained community any more.'

'But it's still a pretty good place to live.' Marshall pushed away his empty coffee-cup, and rose to his feet. 'We never got around to my spare bedrooms, Candy. Would you like to look now? Or do you feel you've seen enough for one day?'

In other circumstances Candy would happily have looked at the bedrooms. But she didn't dare to go upstairs with Marshall again, even to an empty room.

'To be honest, I've seen enough,' she said, with a slightly forced smile. 'I'll have to come back another time and have a look at them.'

'Do, please. Mind, it won't be for a while, I'm afraid.'

'Why, are you going to be in France for long?'

'Till December, I reckon. There's a lot of work to be done on the book, and I've one or two other commissions to sort out while I'm over there. So it'll be near Christmas before I'm back in the village, except perhaps for flying visits to check on the post and grab some new clothes.'

'Well, I hope you have a good trip,' Candy said. She too rose to her feet. 'I really ought to leave you some time to pack.'

'No need, I'm all but finished already. Come through to the sitting-room and listen to some music.'

Candy quietly shook her head. 'I really should be going, Marshall.'

'You're sure? It's still early.'

'Quite sure.'

He frowned, and for a moment she felt sorry she had refused. She wasn't anxious to return to her empty cottage, and she would have enjoyed listening to and talking about Marshall's record collection. But it was a bad idea, she thought, to spend more time alone with him—especially sprawling on the floor by a stereo system!

Though it was barely nine o'clock, she had been at the Hall for hours. So it wasn't rude of her, surely, to insist on leaving. And he surely realised why she was acting as she was?

Perhaps he did, because he didn't persist. He moved towards the door, then turned and said, 'I'd better not take the Porsche, because I've been drinking. Do you mind my walking you home? It's a dry evening, and not too cold. Or if you'd rather, I'll call you a taxi.'

Normally she would gladly have settled for the walk. It wasn't far, and she enjoyed walking. But even that struck her as a dangerous proposition. Walking with Marshall in the moonlight? Being kissed by Marshall on her doorstep? Far too tempting. 'I'd rather take a taxi,' she said awkwardly. And a few minutes later she was switching on the lights in her own empty little cottage.

'Do you realise,' Paul Morland said, over dinner at a Chinese restaurant in Wansham, 'that it'll be Christmas in less than three weeks now?'

'Good heavens, so it will!' Candy gave him a rueful grin. 'At school I realise, Paul; we've had the children practising for their nativity play ever since half-term. But I tend to forget as soon as I walk through my own door. I can't say I've made many personal plans yet.'

'Where do you go for Christmas, Candida?'

'It varies. We're not a family given to great gatherings of the clan, though I've been back to my parents for maybe half the Christmases since I left to go to college. Last year I spent a day with them, and the rest of the holiday in London with a group of friends. And this year—I'm honestly not sure yet.'

'I was wondering if you'd like to come with me, to stay with my family in Yorkshire. It's quite a journey, I know, but it's generally worth it. Mum and Dad always push the boat out for Christmas, and there'll be a dozen or more of us up there.'

'It sounds lovely, Paul. I'm sure you always have a great time. But...'

'But what? You'd be more than welcome, Candida.'

'That's kind of you to say so, Paul. But I feel Christmas ought to be a family occasion.'

Paul reached over the table, and took her hand. 'And you're not one of the family. I know that. But these things have to start somewhere, and I thought... I hoped...'

His voice trailed away, in evident dismay at the expression on Candy's face. Candy gulped, and tried to rearrange it into a more suitable look of gratitude and concern.

'I thought you thought of me as a good friend, Paul,' she said gently.

'I do. You are. But . . .' He changed his mind, and started again, more determinedly. 'And you always will be, Candida, if that's what you'd like to be.'

'I would. I always enjoy seeing you and going out with you, Paul, but perhaps we have been seeing a little too much of each other recently. I hadn't meant to mislead you into thinking that there's any more to it than friendship.'

'Not at all,' Paul said with forced heartiness. 'Now shall we order two coffees, or would you rather go for a drink before closing time?'

Candy drove home from Wansham that evening feeling subdued, and more than a little unhappy. She hadn't meant to be unfair to Paul, but, looking back, she could see that it was no wonder he had misread her intentions. Ever since half-term she had been consciously looking him out: telephoning him a couple of times a week, seeing him every weekend and sometimes during the week as well. Their physical relationship had never progressed beyond a goodnight peck on the cheek, but she knew that most of their acquaintances thought of them as an established couple, and that was hardly surprising.

Even Paul himself wasn't to know that she had been seeing him as much as anything because she wanted to push the thought of Marshall Scott out of her mind. She genuinely did enjoy Paul's company, but she was no nearer desiring him as a lover than she had been on their first meeting, and she couldn't believe that those missing feelings would ever come.

He had made the mildest of advances, and she had done her best to be tactful in her refusal. She felt confident that their friendship would survive the set-back. But at the same time, she could see that she simply couldn't go on seeing Paul as frequently as she had been doing over the previous six weeks.

She would miss him, she thought. And what could she replace those missing evenings out with? There didn't seem any point in looking for another boyfriend, when she knew very well that her feelings weren't free to be bestowed on even the most wonderful of men—unless his name was Marshall Scott.

'I'm falling in love with you,' Marshall had said, the last time she had seen him. Though she hadn't been so rash as to say it out loud herself, she had fallen in love with him too. She couldn't see, though, how there could be any future in a relationship with Marshall. Though things had progressed steadily over the few months they had known each other, he certainly hadn't courted her in any conventional sense. And, from a couple of brief meetings she had had with Caroline, she knew that he was still in contact with the other girl. Caroline never failed to mention her wonderful boyfriend, and the great times they had together.

He's a tiger, she kept telling herself: dangerous, predatory, not to be trusted an inch. Not to be thought about. She really ought to make some arrangements for Christmas. She didn't want to spend a single minute, let alone the best holiday of the year, on her own moping over a man she couldn't have.

The next evening she called round at Juliet's, and came away again with an enthusiastic invitation to spend all of Christmas Day and Boxing Day with her and Peter.

CHAPTER EIGHT

'OH, Miss Harper,' Mrs Kipling said, buttonholing Candy in the school staff-room a couple of days later. 'I only realised yesterday that I'd forgotten to ask you to make the arrangements for the nativity play.'

'It's coming along fine, Mrs Kipling,' Candy said with a smile. 'I'm sure everything will be all right on the night.'

'I'm sure it will. But the thing is to make sure that there will *be* a night. Or rather, a place to hold the night.'

'Oh.' Candy's mind whizzed into top gear. It hadn't occurred to her before, but, now that she stopped to think, it was obvious that the school's small hall-cum-dining-room really wasn't big enough to hold a hundred performing children and their admiring parents, grandparents, and elder brothers and sisters. Little Bixton didn't have a village hall; the old hall had burnt down three years earlier, and the villagers were still fund-raising for its replacement. So where on earth was the nativity play held? In St Margaret's Church? In a hall in Wansham?

'Of course in the Major's day we could take it for granted,' Mrs Kipling was saying, 'though we always went to ask, needless to say. But now that the Hall's changed hands...'

'You hold the play at Little Bixton Hall?' Candy exclaimed.

'That's right—at least, we have for the past three years. There's a big upstairs room that the Major always cleared out for us. We take the chairs up from the school in Mr Watson's van. It's not ideal, but it's the best alternative, we've always found.'

'You don't think the church would be more suitable?'

Mrs Kipling firmly shook her head. 'The vicar doesn't like to hold plays in St Margaret's, and there's nowhere for the children to change, or for the PTA to serve teas in the interval. And the chapel's too small. So it really does have to be the Hall, if you can possibly arrange it.'

'It's my job?'

Mrs Kipling sniffed. 'The teacher in charge of the nativity play has always arranged it.'

Candy silently cursed. Mrs Kipling must have known Marshall since he was knee-high, she thought to herself: surely she could do it herself!

But she swallowed her objections, and said mildly, 'Actually, Mrs Kipling, I'm not sure that Mr Scott is even in the country.'

'Then you'd better speak to Mrs Dobson, hadn't you?' Mrs Kipling gave a tight, triumphant smile, and hurried off before Candy could bring out any more objections.

Candy didn't relish the job, but in fact it proved to cause no difficulty. Mrs Dobson had been housekeeper to the Major before Marshall bought the Hall, so she knew all about the arrangements, and she assured Candy that Marshall couldn't possibly object to the Hall's being used once again. He had lived in Little Bixton all his life, after all, so he had acted in quite a few of the village school nativity plays himself!

A couple of afternoons later Candy drove up to the Hall after school had finished, and she went through everything with Mrs Dobson, agreeing which rooms they would use as changing-rooms, how they would sort out the refreshments, and so on.

A group of fathers on the PTA would shift out the armchairs and sofas from the upstairs sitting-room, and set out the folding chairs that the school normally kept in store. Candy hesitated over the Scandinavian pictures. She felt that Marshall might have preferred to have them taken down and stored elsewhere in safety, rather than subjecting them to the attention of a couple of hundred parents and children. Mrs Dobson was adamant, though, that he would object strongly to having them moved in his absence, so they finally agreed to leave them all on the walls.

Candy asked about Marshall, and Mrs Dobson told her that he wasn't intending to return to Little Bixton before Christmas Eve. The nativity play would be held on the twenty-second, with a dress rehearsal the day before. So there would be time not only to get it all out of the way, but to clear up perfectly and make amends for any damage before he even knew about the arrangements.

Ten days later, a neat crocodile of small children, shepherded by Candy and by half a dozen willing mothers, wound their way through Little Bixton, along Whiskey Lane, and up the drive of Little Bixton Hall. Mrs Dobson greeted them at the front door, and assured Candy that Blitzen had been locked away in the garden-room. They all trailed up the staircase, and Candy stationed herself at the top to direct them to the rooms they would use to change into their costumes for the dress rehearsal.

She left the mothers to start on the costumes, and went alone into the long room. In front of her,

Richard Bergh's beautiful painting of the girl on the terrace seemed to breathe restfulness and calm. I'll need a little of that, Candy thought to herself: persuading a hundred children to stand in the right places, let alone to sing in time with each other and to speak their few lines of dialogue, would take all the energy she possessed and more!

A moment later the first of the angels had burst in through the door, and been pointed to where she was to stand. In next to no time the horde of children were all standing in neat rows, and loudly singing the first verse of 'While Shepherds Watched' while Candy banged the old piano to try and make a noise that they would hear above the din of their own voices.

Joseph forgot a couple of his lines, and Mary dropped the doll that was serving as Baby Jesus, but on the whole it went smoothly, and the mothers and Mrs Dobson were full of oohs and aahs at the back of the room. Candy leaped from the piano stool and nudged the children into their final tableau. Then she rushed back, and struck up the first chords of 'Away in a Manger'.

'What the hell is going on here?'

At the first sound of a loud, and extremely angry—and all too familiar—male voice, Candy went cold. She tried to play a couple more chords, but her fingers had turned to thumbs. She gave up trying, rose to her feet as the children's voices faded away behind her, and found herself transfixed by Marshall Scott's glare, undiminished in its intensity by the distance it had to travel across the room.

'Candy! What on earth are you doing here? What the hell is all this in aid of?'

Candy took a deep breath.

'It's the dress rehearsal for the school nativity play, Mr Scott.' As you can see perfectly well, she added under her breath. 'I—I didn't think you were coming back till Christmas Eve.'

'Didn't you? Didn't you?' Marshall stepped forwards till he was less than an arm's length from where Candy stood by the piano. 'Am I to take it that you planned to drag the whole of Little Bixton here without my even finding out?'

'I'd have asked your permission if you were here to ask.'

'And since I wasn't, you simply assumed that you had it!'

Candy's own temper flared at the injustice of that. 'That's not so!' she retorted furiously. 'I did my best to make sure that everything would be OK with you. But I certainly didn't imagine that you'd refuse!'

'You didn't? You didn't! You imagined I wanted a great horde of small kids tramping through my house and putting their sticky fingers all over my possessions! You imagined I wanted their parents and grandparents and God knows who else roaming all over the place! I bet you didn't even check on the insurance!'

'I *imagined*, Mr Scott, that you'd be happy to agree for the school to do what we've done year after year, without anything but encouragement and co-operation from the owner of Little Bixton Hall. But I obviously *imagined* wrong. So don't you worry about your precious paintings and photographs and your crummy old Hall. We'll go and do our nativity play somewhere else!'

Candy ended this speech on the sort of crescendo that really demanded that she march out instantly. But she couldn't march out until a hundred children were ready to march with her, so she hadn't any option but to fix Marshall with her angriest, most determined look, and try to simply stare him out.

He held her eye for a long, agonising moment: long enough to tell her that his will was considerably more than a match for hers. Then, just as she was starting to feel that she ought perhaps to have taken a more conciliatory approach, he snapped, 'You do just that!' He swung round, to distribute a share of his glaring look to the mothers and Mrs Dobson; then he strode back towards the door, where they backed away instinctively to clear a path for him, and out of the room.

Candy didn't stop to think, or she might have collapsed in shock. She shouted at the mothers, 'Well, what are you waiting for? Let's get out of here!'

They didn't need asking twice. A bare twenty minutes later, the confused but excited children, half of them still in their costumes, and their subdued supervisors were making their way back down Whiskey Lane. And as they left Little Bixton Hall, Marshall Scott was absolutely nowhere to be seen.

By the time she was halfway down Whiskey Lane, Candy knew that she had been a fool. Marshall's reaction hadn't really been so unreasonable, if he hadn't known at all about the nativity play. He had had a valid point about the insurance; she hadn't checked on it, and she was willing to bet Mrs Dobson hadn't either. She should have appeased him, she knew, flattered and pleaded, and he might have relented.

But it was too late now; she had already walked out, and she couldn't turn round and walk a hundred children back again. She reassured the mothers that she would easily find an alternative venue for the play—though she wasn't nearly as confident of that as she pretended to be—and concentrated on racking her brains for possibilities.

It will just have to be the church, she thought. Maybe the children can change at the school and hurry across the road in their costumes. Or maybe Bill will let us use the big bar at the Poacher's Pocket; after all, lots of the parents are his regular customers! Or if those won't do, maybe Mrs Kipling will agree to lean on Marshall. She might well succeed where I failed.

She tried to shrug off the difficulty when she reached the school again, though Mrs Kipling soon got to hear what had happened, and came rushing to Candy's classroom to question her.

'I'll sort it out this evening, Mrs Kipling,' Candy assured her.

'You'll have to,' Mrs Kipling said ominously. 'The play's tomorrow, and we can't postpone it now that all the invitations have gone out.'

Candy rushed home when the school day finished, and got out her telephone directory. She was just reaching out to pick up the receiver and ring the vicar when the phone rang.

'Candy Harper,' she said cautiously, half expecting to find an angry mother on the other end of the line.

'Candy, it's Marshall.'

'Oh.' Candy's mind began to race. 'Marshall, look, I'm awfully sorry,' she began in a rush, before Marshall could say anything else. 'It was stupid of me not to think about the insurance. And I'd have asked you before you left for France if only I'd known about the play then, but Mrs Kipling didn't tell *me* until a couple of weeks ago.'

'OK, OK,' Marshall said. 'I'm sorry too. I'd only just got home after a fifteen-hour journey, and the phone hasn't stopped ringing since!'

'I'm sorry,' Candy repeated. 'Look, I've got some ideas for where else we might go, and the crisis will be over in no time, I'm sure——'

'For heaven's sake,' Marshall interrupted, 'you'll have to come here. It's far too late to change the venue.'

'But the insurance... the pictures...'

'We'll sort it out as best we can. Heavens, I don't want to offend the entire village! I'll move the pictures up to the loft; there's a lock on my workroom door. I've already phoned the insurance company.'

'Marshall, that's really kind of you.'

'There's no alternative,' Marshall said bluntly.

'Can I help? With moving the pictures, or...'

'No need: Jack's coming up in half an hour to do it with me. You concentrate on smoothing all the ruffled feathers, and I'll see you at the Hall tomorrow evening.'

The lights blazed in the windows of Little Bixton Hall the following evening, and the drive and forecourt were solid with cars and with shouting, laughing parents and children. Candy peered out of the window of the 'changing-room'—one of the empty bedrooms—and watched all the activity down below.

This is what a house like this should be like, she thought to herself. It makes a wonderful home for Marshall, true: but a grand old house needs lots of people to make it come alive. I do hope he gets married soon and sets about filling it—even if it is to Caroline Greenwood.

'Everything under control?'

Marshall's quiet voice, just to the side of her, made her jump; she hadn't realised he had come into the room.

'I think so,' she agreed. 'There's a boot brigade at the door, to make sure nobody trails mud into the house. We've roped off all the corridors that are out of bounds, and turned off the lights so that nobody will be tempted to go in the wrong direction. There are signs on all the doors. And the tea urn's working perfectly for once: fancy a cup?'

'I think I need something stronger than that. Join me in a glass of sherry?'

Candy shook her head. 'Afterwards I'd love one, but I'll need an absolutely clear head to keep all the children under control.'

'Then I won't encourage you. We don't want them to wreck the joint, do we?'

'Marshall,' Candy said. 'I haven't had a chance to say yet, but it really is good of you to let us go ahead. I know it's not what you wanted to happen at all. Now I can see that it was stupid of me to take it for granted that you'd approve of our coming here.'

'Mrs Dobson told me that you always come here.'

'That's true. But you're not the Major, and——'

'But I'm part of Little Bixton,' Marshall firmly interrupted. 'I'm trying to become a better part of it, too. Help me, please, Candy. I can manage it if you help me, I know I can.'

What on earth did he mean? Candy didn't understand at all. Then a voice from outside the door called out, 'Miss Harper! Can we start changing now?' and Marshall moved a pace back, murmuring,

'I'd better beat a hasty retreat.'

'Just a moment,' Candy shouted. 'Marshall, I'll talk to you afterwards. OK, children, let's get going now.'

* * *

Candy gestured, waved and mouthed instructions: Mary and Joseph shuffled into place, with the shepherds and wise men around them, and a huge company of angels and people at the inn behind them. Mary held the doll with exaggerated care; she hadn't dropped it once. Candy nodded her approval, struck up the first chords of the final hymn, and all the audience rose to their feet.

Three hundred voices, young and old, sang out the familiar words of 'Away in a Manger'. After all the difficulties, all the patient persuasion and the encouragement and the occasional despair, Candy's heart lifted in the knowledge that her nativity play was a huge and indisputable success.

The last notes faded away, and there was a short, a very short silence before everybody began to talk at once.

'Just a moment, please,' the headmistress called out. 'The vicar would like us to join him in a short prayer, and then Mr Scott, who is our host tonight, has something to say before we leave.'

The vicar's prayer was mercifully short. 'Amen,' the massed voices all repeated, and then he gave way to Marshall at the front of the room.

'I won't keep you a minute,' Marshall said. 'I'd just like to thank you all for being my guests at Little Bixton Hall tonight, and to wish you all a very merry Christmas. You'll have seen the signs pointing the way to the room where the ladies of the PTA will be serving tea in a couple of minutes. Mrs Dobson, my housekeeper, has baked a bumper batch of mince pies, so there's a mince pie for everyone to go with your tea. Thank you, children, for a wonderful play; thank you, Miss Harper, for arranging it; and that's all.'

Marshall stepped away from the front as soon as these last words were out of his mouth, and disappeared through a side door. He found it hard to say that, Candy thought. He can't enjoy speaking in public one bit. He did it perfectly, though. What on earth did he mean about needing me to help him? It seems to me that he doesn't need any help at all.

She half rose to her feet, thinking for a second of going after him, until common sense told her that she would be needed just where she was. Then a dozen people crowded round her to echo Marshall's thanks, and there was no possibility of escape.

Even after the adults had released her, Candy had to supervise the children as they changed out of their costumes. And then the vicar cornered her, and enthused over the performance too.

'I'm glad you liked it, Vicar,' Candy said abstractedly, searching the room to see if Marshall had reappeared.

'Oh, admirable, my dear. I must admit, after the village fête I did wonder whether Mrs Kipling had taken on the right person, but I can see now that she did!'

'The village fête? I don't understand, Vicar.'

'All that mumbo-jumbo over the fortune-telling. I know half my parishioners read their horoscopes, but it's pagan rubbish, really, and I don't like to encourage it.'

'So it was you!'

'It was me? I don't follow, dear. Oh, yes, just a moment . . .'

He patted her arm and disappeared. And Candy, sighing over how easy it was to misread people, made her way to the refreshments room.

Marshall wasn't there either, and she was soon monopolised by yet another group of parents and children. It took her a good ten minutes to ease away from their congratulations, and she had barely taken two steps away from them before Mrs Kipling appeared.

'Ah, Candy. Just the person I wanted to see. You have a car, don't you? I told Mrs Jones and Mrs Mortimer that you would be able to give them a lift back into the village. Mrs Mortimer's feeling a little dizzy, so you'd better run along right away.'

Candy knew Mrs Mortimer, an elderly lady renowned for groaning about her ailments. 'I would, Mrs Kipling,' she said, 'but there's plenty still to be done here. I've got to fold the costumes, and sort out the clearing up, and...'

'Don't worry about that,' Mrs Kipling said briskly. 'The PTA ladies will see to all that.'

'But I wanted to thank Mr Scott, and...'

'I'll thank him, don't you worry. Mrs Mortimer's in the hall, waiting for you.'

But, but, but! Curse Mrs Kipling! She couldn't persist any more. And even if she did, she couldn't have left all the PTA ladies to clear up while she dashed after Marshall to find out what was going on in that complicated mind of his. She muttered, 'OK, Mrs Kipling,' and hurried down to the hall.

Marshall had forgiven her, she felt sure. All evening she had been conscious of his glances, his occasional smiles. He had as good as said as much. There still seemed to be a thousand questions to be asked, though, and a thousand things to be sorted out between the two of them.

For all his occasional kisses and loving words to her, he was still the man Caroline was crazy about.

Candy didn't trust his attraction to her, which seemed to be unnervingly on-and-off, and though she was finding him hard to resist she was genuinely scared at the prospect of becoming his lover. What if he did love her briefly, and then went back to Caroline afterwards? How would she cope if that happened?

The more she thought about it, the more she was tempted to leave any new confrontation with him until after Christmas. On the day after the nativity play, though, Mrs Kipling delivered a bottle of whisky and ordered her to present it to him as a thank-you present from the school PTA.

That's it, Candy thought. I've got to see him, even if it does mean that I end up crying into Juliet's arms all Christmas through. She picked what she hoped would be a suitable time—seven o'clock in the evening—and set off in her little car to the Hall.

It had been a dull, icy day. The weather forecasters had been talking of a white Christmas, but there wasn't any snow to be seen: just the remnants of that morning's frost, which still hadn't evaporated as there had been so little sun.

Mrs Dobson opened the door to her.

'Is Mr Scott in?' Candy asked.

'No, he's not, lovey. He was asked to a drinks party the other side of Wansham, and I'm not expecting him back till eight or later. Was it something important?'

'Just to thank him, and to give him this from the PTA.'

'Would you like to wait? Or shall I tell him you'll call back later?'

Candy thought for a moment, then said, 'I think I'll just write him a note. But do tell him I'm sorry to have missed him.'

Mrs Dobson found her some paper, and she carefully wrote a short, and fairly impersonal, thank-you letter to Marshall. She folded it in two, stood the bottle of whisky on top, and stood back with Mrs Dobson to admire her handiwork.

'He should be back this evening for certain,' Mrs Dobson assured her. 'So he'll see it then, dear.'

'Thanks, Mrs Dobson. And a happy Christmas to you.'

Mrs Dobson insisted that the two of them drink a sherry together before Candy left. Candy didn't ask about Marshall's plans, but Mrs Dobson told her anyway that he wasn't intending to stay at the Hall over Christmas; he would be visiting relatives, she thought, while she herself would be going to stay with her married daughter.

Then I most likely won't see him again over the holiday, Candy thought to herself as she drove back to her cottage. That's as well, really it is.

Back home, she stoked up the real fire that she had lit to supplement her central heating, put the stirring tones of Handel's *Messiah* on to her record player, made herself a strong cup of coffee, and set about wrapping the last of her Christmas presents.

She was on to side three of the *Messiah*, and there was a neat pile of prettily wrapped and ribboned presents piled up on the floor, when the doorbell rang.

'Let me in, quick,' a familiar voice said, as soon as she had the latch open. 'It's just starting to snow out there; it's the most diabolical evening.'

'Marshall!' Heavens, was she pleased to see him! She flung the door wide open, and would have flung her arms around him too if he hadn't dashed in quickly, and ordered her in a very prosaic voice to shut it fast behind him before she froze the whole house out.

She did this, then turned to see him standing in the centre of her living-room, wearing a thick grey greatcoat, with flecks of snow just melting on its shoulders and among the dark mass of his hair. Their eyes met, and Candy's insides melted. He loves me, she thought. No, he doesn't. How can he, when he loves Caroline?

'You've just driven back from Wansham?' she said in as cool and normal a voice as she could manage.

'Three miles the other side, and there's black ice on the roads the whole way.'

'You'll need some coffee, then.'

Marshall shook his head. 'Something stronger. I left the Porsche up at the Hall, and I plan to walk home, so I'm free to drink tonight. I brought this with me, since I know you never keep drink in your house.'

He held out a bottle of vintage port. 'I didn't like to bring the whisky back,' he said, 'in case you'd misinterpret the gesture.'

'It wasn't from me, it's from the PTA. But port's fine; hold on, I'll just get a couple of glasses.'

By the time she returned from the kitchen Marshall had thrown off his sodden overcoat, settled down on her new sofa, and was taking off his boots.

'You'll have to forgive bare feet,' he said, looking up with a smile. 'I'll put these by the fire to dry out, if I may.'

'Do, and put your feet there too,' Candy said. Marshall promptly obeyed, stretching out his long legs in front of him. Candy could see the last snowflakes melting on his trousers: it obviously was a really unpleasant night.

'I doubt if it'll be a white Christmas,' he said. 'The weathermen are predicting a rise in temperature tomorrow, so we'll have a slushy Christmas instead.'

'How delicious.' Candy knelt down by the fire, poured the port, and handed him a glass.

'This is cosy,' he said, taking a sip and looking round approvingly. 'Something's changed since I was last here.'

'The sofa,' Candy said with a laugh, remembering how he had teased her about the packing cases. 'I bought it with the help of my modelling fee.'

'Oh, yes.' He gave a rueful smile. 'I still feel guilty over those photographs. All that work, and nothing to show for it.'

'There's the sofa to show for it.'

'There's that, true. But all the same, I want to take some more photos of you as soon as you'll let me.'

'Marshall,' Candy said patiently, 'I really don't like having my photo taken.'

'I won't be as bad-tempered next time, I promise.'

'It's not that. It's just that—well, I don't particularly like the way I look.'

'You don't l——' He broke off in mid word, considered for a moment, then went on, 'No, you don't, do you?'

'I'm not paranoid about it, honestly. It doesn't ruin my life not to be a stunning blonde with legs up to my armpits. But since I'm not, why encourage the world to look at me?'

'Because you're beautiful, you little idiot!'

'I'm not!'

'I think you are. Honestly I do. You could make more of yourself if you had a little more confidence, but the raw material is all there.'

Candy opened her mouth to protest, then she shut it again, and thought instead.

It was funny, but she really didn't feel as plain now as she had felt in those grey days after Andrew had left her. Then it had seemed to her that no sane man would ever choose a dark little scrap like her, not while the world was full of tall, stunning blondes. But one way and another, what with Paul Morland's gentle flattery, and Marshall's intermittent attentions, and the sheer healing effect of time, that desolate feeling had gone.

'The weird thing is,' she said slowly, 'that I almost believe you.'

'Why not? It's the truth.'

'Because—oh, mainly because of a man. He was always a critical type, and when he left me he really rubbed it in, and made me feel like the most unattractive girl in the whole world.'

'You're certainly not that,' Marshall said with a short laugh.

'I know! Mind you, I know I'm not the greatest beauty either, and never will be. But I'm over Andrew now, really over him, and now I honestly can believe that one day I'll make some man love the way I look.'

'Paul Morland?'

'Paul Morland!' The suggestion surprised her so much that she laughed out loud. 'Paul's a nice guy, but I don't want him to love me, for heaven's sake!'

'But I thought...'

He thought—what? Candy turned wide eyes on him, took in his edgy, uncertain expression, and suddenly knew just what he had thought.

'Oh, no,' she said gently. 'Paul's a good friend, Marshall, but he's never been more than that.'

Slowly, slowly, Marshall's eyes came round to meet hers.

Somehow, without quite knowing how, they found themselves in each other's arms on the carpet. Candy was underneath, with the warm, solid bulk of Marshall's body shielding her from the fire. His mouth was on hers, his hands were roving over her, loving, possessing, and her hands sought for and found the firm planes of his shoulders and back, caressing and moulding him to her.

'You wouldn't believe how jealous I've been of Paul Morland,' he whispered.

'There's no need to be. None at all,' she murmured back.

'Not while you're here with me.' The last words were almost lost as he buried his face in the loose mass of her hair.

Here, here with him. Candy's body was starting to burn with pleasure. She was beautiful, she knew she was. Weren't Marshall's hands, Marshall's mouth, telling her so every moment? He did love the way she looked, and with him loving her how could she fail to be beautiful? As beautiful as he was. She responded with growing hunger, slipping her own hands underneath his jumper and feeling the smooth skin that seemed to flow across the muscles of his back.

'That's better,' Marshall whispered, as his mouth moved a fraction away from hers. 'Much better.' He moved a little, bringing one of his legs in between hers, and easing the weight on her a little. His mouth touched hers again in a series of kisses, butterfly light. 'Happy Christmas, Candy darling,' he murmured.

'Happy Christmas, Marshall,' Candy whispered back. This was what she wanted for Christmas, she thought dreamily. For Marshall to hold her, kiss her, make love to her.

Somewhere at the back of her mind, the thought began to push forward that this was not at all what she had intended. That maybe Marshall had no reason to be jealous of Paul but she still had plenty of reason to be jealous of Caroline. Not now . . . not now he was here with her. But what about afterwards, when he left her and returned to his regular girlfriend? 'Marshall,' she murmured, 'I don't think we . . .'

'Yes, we do,' Marshall replied. He put a finger to her lips, gently silencing her. 'You do want me, I know you do.'

'But . . .'

'No buts.'

His mouth now was hard, determined and confident. His tongue thrust into her mouth, setting up an assertive, seductive rhythm. His hand reached down to the hem of her sweater, pushing it upwards and drawing soft patterns on the bare skin underneath.

Candy closed her eyes and luxuriated in the sheer pleasure of his caresses. His hand claimed her breast, and then moved behind her to locate and unfasten the catch of her bra. She caught her breath at the touch of his fingers, teasing and arousing her nipple into a peak of hard, aching pleasure.

She sighed with delight. Her hands roved across the broad expanse of Marshall's back, bunching near the base of his spine and pressing him to her. He moved slightly to align their hips, and she could feel the hardness of his arousal, nudging gently against her thigh.

She had to have him, had to. Maybe it would hurt afterwards. Maybe it would hurt Caroline as well, but there weren't any decisions to be made about it any more. The time for choice was far behind them.

Marshall moved again, slipping his fingers inside the waistband of her jeans, caressing the soft skin of her abdomen. He unbuttoned her jeans, deftly, one-handed, and pulled the zip downwards. Candy quivered with desire. Each one of her nerve-endings seemed to flare into life a second before Marshall's hand passed over it. Every touch was so delicious it was almost unbearable, because it made her want more, and more, and more.

She arched her body upwards and clutched at his shoulders as his skilful, gentle hands guided her body up a mountain of desire. His fingers found the moist core of her, and her own fingernails dug into his shoulders until he groaned out loud.

'Marshall,' she whispered in amazed delight at what he was doing to her.

'You do want me,' Marshall whispered hoarsely. 'You do. I love you, Candy. I never thought I'd say that, not to any woman, but I'm saying it now to you. Candy, I love you.'

'I love you too.'

He was scrambling now to remove his own clothes, and Candy hurriedly pulled off what was left of hers. Then his body was reclaiming hers, skin to skin this time. She could feel the warmth of the fire on his side. His mouth moved downwards again, lower and lower, and his teeth nipped gently at the super-sensitive skin of her inner thighs. Candy's insides seemed to dissolve into an aching vacuum. She had never felt so overwhelmed by desire. But she wasn't blinded; she seemed to be more acutely alive, more conscious of every tiny touch and movement than she had ever been before.

'Now?' Marshall whispered, bringing his face close to hers, aligning their bodies, fixing her with his look.

She held his eyes. They met hers unflinchingly, and she seemed to be looking down, down, into the very depths of him. This couldn't be wrong, surely. He was her man, hers beyond doubt. There could no more be anyone else for him than there was for her. He loved her, and she loved him.

'Now.'

For a moment that seemed to Candy like an eternity he didn't move at all. Then, with calm, confident certainty, he joined the two of them.

All of Candy, inside and out, seemed to clutch at him, tightening and completing their union. For a moment they were still once more, and then Marshall was moving, steadily, rhythmically, and she was moving under him, and the swell of desire was escalating into an avalanche which swept over her and carried her away into a place of blind ecstasy.

Afterwards they lay silently, wrapped in each other's arms, bathed by the warmth of the fire, for a long time. Candy still felt dizzy and amazed. She had thought she knew about love from her time with Andrew, but with Andrew it had never, never been like this.

'I'll have to go soon,' Marshall said quietly.

'Can't you stay tonight?'

'Better not. Mrs Dobson will wonder where I am, and I have to get off early in the morning. I'm spending Christmas with an aunt and uncle on the other side of London, and I promised to get there by lunchtime tomorrow.'

'I'm spending mine with Juliet and Peter,' Candy murmured. She snuggled even closer to him. She didn't want him to go yet. Everything, everyone but

Marshall, seemed to have receded into the far distance. With the sheer exhilarating pleasure of their lovemaking, everything seemed to have fallen into place. She knew there were lots of questions still to be asked and answered, but somehow they didn't seem important any more. Marshall loved her and she loved him. Those were the only things that were really important.

'You're getting cold,' he said quietly. 'Shall I put some more coal on the fire? Or will you be going to bed pretty soon?'

'I'm sleepy, but don't go yet. Stay as long as you can.'

'Let me take you to bed.'

He stood up, and pulled her to her feet, gently. Then his arms went around her, and she found herself being lifted up, held firmly against him. She slipped her own arms around his neck and he carried her, still naked, up the narrow stairs and into her bedroom. He let her down gently on her bed, and saw her under the covers. 'Don't come down again,' he said. 'I'll see to everything downstairs.' His mouth touched hers for one last time, fleetingly, then he made for the door.

Candy lay in her cool bed, sleepily aware of the light being turned off, of the little noises of Marshall making his way downstairs and seeing to the fire. Before the gentle thud of the front door came, she was fast asleep.

The next afternoon a florist from Wansham, driving through the slush, delivered a large bouquet of Christmas roses to Candy's doorstep. 'Happy Christmas, dear,' she said, handing them over.

Marshall's card said the same. Happy Christmas. Love from Marshall.

Candy arranged them in a vase on her mantelpiece, and spent the rest of the day with Juliet, helping her sister with her final preparations and entertaining the children. She had decided it would be better to leave Juliet and Peter alone together that evening, so she spent it in the Poacher's Pocket, with a crowd of her neighbours. Afterwards most of them went on to St Margaret's for midnight mass.

After the lovely candlelit service, Candy walked home with Mr and Mrs Watson, and to her surprise—and pleasure—they invited her in for a glass of sherry afterwards.

'We did enjoy your nativity play, Candy,' Mrs Watson said. 'So lovely those angels looked, and you played the piano a treat.'

'I'm out of practice really,' Candy demurred. 'I don't have a piano of my own in the cottage, so I only play for music classes at school.'

'You want to see if you can go up to the Hall sometimes and use Marshall's.'

'Perhaps I shall.'

'We've noticed Marshall's Porsche outside your cottage once or twice, so we know you've got friendly with him. I shouldn't call him Marshall these days, I suppose, it ought to be Mr Scott now, but old habits die hard, you know.'

'I'm sure he doesn't mind.'

'I wouldn't be sure myself,' Mrs Watson went on with hardly a pause. 'He always was a prickly lad. Still is in some ways, specially where the past's concerned. Now, seeing him welcome everybody to his house, that was a real surprise to us. Jack and I, we never thought he'd do it.'

They never thought he'd do it! But why? Why hadn't everyone expected Marshall to act like part of the village? Why had Marshall himself said that he needed her help? Candy couldn't understand it.

'I thought everybody took it for granted,' she said. 'Mrs Kipling told me the Hall was used for the nativity play when the Major lived there.'

'Oh, yes, but you know, young Marshall's a different type entirely. He always likes to keep to himself. Even when he lived just over the road here he hardly ever asked anybody in. He was always polite enough when you met him, but edgy, you know.'

'I think I do.'

'He had such a chip on his shoulder about his mum and dad, you know. Jack and I always used to say, it'll take the love of a good woman to get him over it. And maybe we were right.'

Maybe Mrs Watson saw far too much! Candy thought with a sudden rush of embarrassment. She hadn't told Juliet a thing about Marshall yet, but maybe she had better hurry, before Mrs Watson spread it all round the village! Hadn't she been warned a dozen times that you couldn't keep anything secret in Little Bixton?

She looked down at her glass until she could feel her blush subsiding, then she said, 'Really I don't see why he should have minded so much about his parents. I know they weren't rich, but then lots of people aren't rich. That's nothing to be ashamed of.' Anyway, she thought to herself, Marshall isn't snobbish at all from what I've seen of him.

'Oh, it's not that, dear.' Mrs Watson set down her glass and leaned closer. 'Old Mr Scott was a very difficult man. He used to bully that lad something terrible. He always wanted Marshall to go and work on Bates' farm. Couldn't stand the idea of him becoming a photographer. One time he burned all the lad's photographs on a bonfire in the back garden. Namby-pamby rubbish, he called them. He thought Marshall should have been a farm labourer like him. His mother thought different, but she never had a say in that household. And in the end——' Mrs Watson leaned closer still, and continued in a stage whisper '—she got to be very fond of the bottle.'

Candy went cold. Marshall bullied and ridiculed; Marshall having his photographs burned—and the whole village knowing about it. Half of her wanted to know more, and the other half felt that even to know this much was a terrible invasion of his privacy. But she had to know, and after the previous night she surely had the right to know. 'How dreadful,' she whispered.

'Oh, it's common enough,' Mrs Watson said matter-of-factly, sitting back in her chair again. 'Isn't it, Jack? But it didn't do young Marshall any good, you can be sure. We always used to say, that's a lad who'll be off and away as soon as ever he can. And I think he would have been, if it hadn't been for the accident. You heard about the accident, dear?'

'Yes,' Candy said in a low voice.

'I won't say it was a blessing in disguise, because you should never say that, should you, dear? But it did bring Marshall back here. He kept to himself, mind, even in those days, but we all knew that was what he was like, so we never pushed him. We used to say, in the end he'll come round. I always thought in a way he was keen to fit in, keen to belong to the place. Otherwise he'd never have stayed, would he?'

'I'm sure he is,' Candy said.

'And that's why we were so pleased to see him saying welcome to everybody. It's not easy for him, you know. He knows people remember.'

'I think I see.'

'Everybody's real proud of him round here. But I think he feels sometimes that they all see him as John Scott's lad who used to get thrashed every Saturday night. He can't see that we all think a lot of him for how he's got over it, what he's made of himself.'

'That we do,' Jack Watson seconded.

'I'm sure you do.' So do I, Candy thought silently. I love him. And slowly, slowly, I feel I'm beginning to understand the man I love.

But she had already stayed longer than she had intended, and found out more than she could easily absorb at once. So she downed the dregs of her sherry and said brightly, 'I really must be getting back home, Mrs Watson. It was so kind of you to ask me in. A very happy Christmas to you both.'

'And you, dear,' the Watsons chorused, as she shook hands and made her way to their front door.

CHAPTER NINE

CANDY was aching to see Marshall again. She didn't only want to make love with him again—though she was more than eager for that—but even more, she wanted to talk to him about Mr and Mrs Watson's revelations.

It seemed to her that at last she had uncovered the key to all his prickliness and uncertainty. Surely his unhappy childhood explained why he had kept himself aloof from people in the village?

Even more, it explained his behaviour to her. It must have left him with a reluctance to make deep commitments. It wasn't sexual intrigue he was unfamiliar with, she thought to herself; doubtless he was only too used to that, but he had probably always shied away from love, from letting things get too serious. That surely was the reason why he had remained unmarried into his thirties. That must have been the reason why he had carried on seeing Caroline as well as her—at least, surely, until that wonderful evening when they had become lovers.

Could he have ever been deeply committed to Caroline, she wondered—even though maybe Caroline had tried to persuade herself that he was? He would never have told Caroline, too, that he loved her, because Candy knew now that that was the hardest thing in the world for him to do. Probably his relationship with the other girl had meant no more to him than hers with Paul Morland had done to her.

And then, when he had dared to tell her of his love, how had she rewarded him? Not by telling him of hers in return, but by doing her best to hold him at arm's length! It would have been so much better if she had told him why she felt guilty and uncertain, but she had been so jealous of Caroline that she had never been able to face doing so.

That had to be the truth—that, or something very like it. She could ask him now. And he would surely explain everything to her as soon as he returned from his aunt's. She sailed through Christmas and Boxing Day, so happy that she didn't even mind the wait for the phone to ring. Then on the day after Boxing Day it did ring. And it was Marshall, but only to say that he had been called away on an urgent project, and he wouldn't be back in Little Bixton until just into the New Year.

'Oh, Marshall,' she wailed.

'I know, darling. It's the last thing I wanted, too, but I really haven't any option. It won't be for too long; I'll be home about the third of January.'

'I'll mark it down on my new calendar,' she assured him.

A couple of days later, she had a phone call from Paul Morland.

'Are you busy on New Year's Eve, Candida?' he asked.

'I'd thought of going over to the Poacher's Pocket,' Candy answered. 'Bill tells me they always have a party there.'

'But you haven't promised? I ran into June a couple of days ago, and she asked me to invite you to her and Philip's New Year party. She didn't have your number, she said, or she'd have rung you herself. You remember June; you met her at that big party back in October?'

'Of course I remember June,' Candy agreed. 'How thoughtful of her to ask me, Paul. You're going yourself, of course?'

'Of course.'

'Could I give you a lift?'

'I think I owe you one this time,' Paul cheerfully replied. 'Shall I call for you at around ten? Oh, it's fancy dress, so you'd better get out your needle and cotton.'

The invitation cheered Candy. It wouldn't be the same as spending New Year's Eve with Marshall, but at least it would keep her busy while she waited for his return. The dismal cold, wet weather had continued right through the holidays, and with her cottage finished, and her schoolwork all up to date, she had been finding it difficult to know what to do with herself.

She spent a happy wet afternoon creating an Egyptian goddess costume out of complex folds of old sheeting and gold paper, and a pleasant evening practising a dramatic black and red make-up to go with it.

'Heavens,' said Paul, when he came to collect her on New Year's Eve, 'I didn't know I was taking Cleopatra to the party!'

'Wrong Egyptian,' Candy corrected him, laughing. 'I'm supposed to be the goddess Isis. And you're...no, don't tell me, I ought to guess. A soldier. Napoleon, perhaps?'

'Wrong side,' Paul teased. 'It's the boots that give it away.'

'Of course, you're Wellington! I should have asked you earlier, then I could have dressed as Lady Wellington.'

'I think I'd have done better to dress up as Tutankhamun,' Paul joked, starting his car. 'I bet yours will be the best costume, Candida, though June herself always makes a big effort.'

'Will it be a large party?'

'Not too big, maybe thirty or forty of us. There's a regular set: June and Philip, Tracy and Bill, Maggie and George; Caroline, of course—but she won't be there this evening, I shouldn't think——'

'Why not?' Candy interrupted.

'Didn't you know? I thought you'd have heard by now: she announced her engagement on Christmas Eve.'

Candy went cold.

'I haven't seen Caroline for weeks,' she managed to say.

'I guess she's been otherwise occupied,' Paul said with a light laugh. 'Her fiancé's away a good deal, but they're more or less inseparable when he's around. We'd all been expecting an engagement some time shortly. Now we'll have to nag Caroline to hold a good engagement party!'

'You certainly shall,' Candy murmured.

It's not such a shock, she tried to tell herself. You knew how Caroline felt; you guessed it was going to happen. Even the Chinese Oracle told you that Marshall would get married very shortly. Up to ten days ago you had taken it for granted that he was Caroline's man. Maybe you tried to persuade yourself for a little while that he wasn't, but you obviously got that very, very wrong. So now you've got to go back,

back to that time when you managed to endure the knowledge that he belonged to somebody else.

But then, everything had been different. Then, she and Marshall hadn't been lovers. Then, Marshall had never told her that it was her—and only her—that he loved.

On Christmas Eve, too! That was just one day after Marshall had called round at her cottage.

The skunk! she thought bitterly. The rotten two-timing skunk! Maybe he had meant it to be a last fling before giving up his bachelorhood, but even so, what a low-down, disgusting thing to do!

It wasn't just for her own sake that she resented it. Even more, she felt sorry for Caroline, whose new fiancé certainly wasn't all that she imagined him to be.

'Candida?' Paul's low voice cut through her thoughts.

'I'm sorry, Paul, I'm afraid I was miles away.'

'It's nothing important. I was only saying that I'll introduce you to Miles Brunsdon if he's there tonight. Remind me if I forget. He's an accountant, and I think he might be just your type.'

Candy didn't feel in the mood for meeting any men; just then she would happily have consigned the whole lot of them to the lower depths. But she did her best to push the news to the back of her mind, and to respond cheerfully to the rest of Paul's casual banter.

Shortly afterwards they arrived at June and Philip's party, and were welcomed by their hostess fetchingly dressed as a huge brown bear. Philip thrust a glass of wine into Candy's hand, and she took a big gulp of it to take away the sharp edge of the shock she had received.

She was determined not to let anyone see how low she was feeling, and she vamped up her Egyptian role as much as she could, flirting shamelessly with Paul and with Miles—a rather grey character, tall and thin and a little lifeless—and with every other man who passed her way. There was plenty of drink, and she let Philip keep on filling her glass up, and kept on taking good gulps whenever she felt herself becoming just a touch morose.

By half-past eleven she was feeling so merry that she was finding it hard to remember what she had been unhappy about let alone to grieve over it. Philip put on some louder music, and everyone began to dance. Candy danced with Paul and with Miles and with Philip, giggling slightly when she tripped over her own feet.

'It's coming close, folks,' June shouted. 'All make sure your glasses are full for the toasts!'

Somebody thrust a full glass into Candy's hand, and she took a big sip from it before holding it out to be filled again.

'Put the radio on, June,' Philip was calling. The music died, and out across the room came the tones of the BBC announcer, waiting for the chimes of Big Ben.

'...eleven, twelve. Happy New Year, folks!'

'Happy New Year,' Candy echoed, draining her glass in one. Miles pulled at her, and they moved side by side into the circle of people singing 'Auld Lang Syne'.

After that, she didn't remember very much.

Next day Candy woke in her own bed, to an unexpectedly bright morning. Or was it afternoon? she wondered, taking in the fact that her curtains hadn't been drawn.

She reached for her watch on her bedside table, and discovered that it was eleven-forty on New Year's Day. Staggering to her feet and across to the window, she discovered the reason for the brightness; the ground outside was thinly but completely carpeted in snow.

Her head felt thick, and her tongue seemed to have been swapped for a shoebrush. She went downstairs, drank three large glasses of orange juice in quick succession, then returned to her bedroom, drew the curtains shut, and promptly fell asleep again.

When she next woke, it was to the insistent sound of the telephone ringing. She lay there listening to it for a while, then when the ringing didn't stop she hauled herself back out of bed and downstairs, and answered it.

It was Paul.

'I had a feeling you might sleep away the whole day unless I stirred you,' he said.

'Boy, you sound disgustingly cheerful,' Candy groaned.

'I drove you home, remember? Not a drop of anything stronger than Diet Coke passed my lips all evening.'

'I wish I could say the same.'

'I bet you do,' Paul said cruelly.

'Oh, Paul, did I disgrace myself last night?'

'I don't think so,' Paul said, after a moment's consideration. 'You were pretty sozzled, Candida, but then, so were June and Philip and most of the others. You just fell asleep in the corner—around one o'clock, I guess. At two-thirty I woke you to take you home, and you murmured a few things about a certain man of our acquaintance, but I'm a gentleman, and I wasn't listening to you. Then I saw you into your house and up the stairs, and left you to undress and get to bed.'

'Paul, I owe you a big, big favour.'

'I should think supper one evening would do it,' Paul said gaily. 'Anyway, it's a sunny day, so have a wonderful New Year, and don't waste any more of it in bed.'

'Paul,' Candy said slowly, 'if you were a little closer, I'd make the biggest snowball ever and throw it straight at you.'

Paul laughed, and put down the phone.

The first sharp pain was over, but there were more ordeals to face, Candy knew. Sooner or later she was sure to run into both Marshall and Caroline. It wasn't Caroline's fault that Marshall had behaved as he had, and she didn't want Caroline to know what had happened. So she would have to steel herself to greet Caroline pleasantly, and to congratulate her on the engagement. Perhaps they really would have an engagement party, as Paul had suggested. If they did, she would have to accept her invitation, and smile her way through it.

The skunk! she thought to herself, again and again. He's not a tiger, he's a low-down skunk. Mulling over Marshall's actions didn't bring her to feel forgiving in the slightest. It wasn't possible even to invent an explanation that would justify his behaviour, let alone to try to convince herself that it was correct. There was no avoiding it: he had behaved atrociously towards her.

School began again when the ground was still carpeted in snow. The regular routine of work and supper and bed fell back into place, and there was only a hidden sore spot in Candy's heart to remind her of the events of before the holidays.

Marshall rang her on the third of January, a few moments after she returned home from the school.

'I'm back,' he said cheerfully. 'The project's all finished, and now I should be in Little Bixton for a couple of months, putting together the material for the book.'

Candy didn't reply.

'Can I come over now, darling?'

'I'd rather not,' she said in an unsteady voice.

'Or you could come over here, if you prefer. That would be better really, because I want to show you some of the photos I took on my trip. I'll give Mrs Dobson the evening off. Come for supper.'

'I'm afraid I'm busy this evening.'

'Busy?'

There was a long, painful silence.

'Candy,' Marshall said, 'I don't understand. Is there something wrong, darling? What is it?'

'I can't talk about it now.' She put the phone down, hurriedly, only seconds before the tears came flooding out of her.

It rang again, but she picked up the receiver and dropped it without saying a word. And again, but this time she didn't touch the receiver at all, and eventually the rings ended, and there was silence.

Two days later she met Caroline, coming out of Little Bixton Post Office.

'Oh, Candy!' Caroline exclaimed, nipping across the street to buttonhole her. 'It's ages since I've seen you.'

'Quite a while, yes.'

'I wanted to ask you over to the farm for supper again, but I've been so busy these past few weeks.'

'It's I who should have asked you,' Candy said with as much politeness as she could muster.

'Then do! I mean—will you? Is your cottage finished yet? Could I come and look at it some time?'

Candy took a deep breath. 'Come now, if you've a few minutes to spare.'

'I'd love to.'

Candy didn't have to say another word until they got within her door, because Caroline was talking non-stop the whole time. Had Candy heard? She had got engaged! So exciting, wasn't it? She could hardly wait for the wedding day. When they were inside Bell Cottage it was just the same. Caroline dashed from room to room, exclaiming about how well Candy had arranged everything, how prettily she had decorated it.

'Your kitchen's just divine,' she went on, as Candy was making them tea. 'I'd like to have one just like this myself.'

'Then why don't you?' Candy found herself retorting, with just a little too much venom. 'You'll need a new kitchen, won't you?' She couldn't help remembering the vast old-fashioned kitchen at the Hall, with its range and its deep enamel sink. Caroline wouldn't want to do her cooking there, surely? Or perhaps she wouldn't cook; perhaps she and Marshall would keep on Mrs Dobson, and Caroline would be a lady of leisure after their marriage.

'Maybe one day I will,' Caroline said cheerfully. 'But it won't be quite yet, I should think. We'll plan to live in James's bachelor flat for a good couple of years, and, though the kitchen there's nothing to write home about, it won't be our top priority to redo it.'

'James?'

Caroline didn't notice the question. She was in full flood. 'It's in Pimlico,' she went on. 'Nice and central. I hope I'll be able to get a secretarial job in the City, or perhaps the West End. I'd prefer the City, even though it's further to travel. That's where James works, so if I can get a job with a City company we'll be able to go to work together each morning.'

Somebody seemed to have poured a bucketful of butterflies down Candy's back. Her earlier nervousness had turned into a pricking, tickling uncertainty. She couldn't have got things wrong yet again. Or could she?

'What does—James—do, Caroline?'

'Oh, didn't I tell you? I've been such a bore going on about him, I tend to forget that some people don't know absolutely everything yet! He deals in futures in the City. He travels an awful lot, of course, and I can't say I'm keen on being left alone in the flat when he goes away, but it's such a good job. Absolutely the coming field, James says. It's one of those jobs where you can do really well while you're still young, and James thinks . . .'

Candy didn't listen to what James thought. Caroline was chattering away so enthusiastically that she didn't notice her friend's abstracted expression, and while she launched into an extended eulogy on James and his job Candy had a chance to try and fit the pieces together.

James! She had never heard of James before, she could swear she hadn't. It was Marshall she had seen Caroline with, Marshall she had known to be Caroline's boyfriend.

Or had she? What had she really heard? What had she really seen?

She and Caroline had only talked about Caroline's boyfriend a couple of times, on the evening when she had gone to supper at the farm and the few brief occasions on which they had met since. She had been working hard to overcome her jealousy, but she hadn't been in a frame of mind to ask lots of questions. The name James hadn't been mentioned, she was sure. But had the name Marshall been mentioned either?

My boyfriend: that was what Caroline had said. You must meet him. It would have been a silly thing to say, really, if the boyfriend had been Marshall, because Caroline had known that she and Marshall had met at the village fête.

Caroline and Marshall had been together at the village fête. She had heard them talking. But had they said anything loving to each other? Had they really acted like lovers, either there or at the party where she had met them afterwards?

Far from it; they had squabbled. She had even thought in passing how odd it was, after Caroline's raving about her boyfriend and how well they got on together. But she had been concentrating so much on not being jealous of Caroline that she had never stood back and drawn the obvious conclusion. Caroline's wonderful boyfriend wasn't Marshall after all.

'You *will* come, won't you, Candy?' Caroline was saying eagerly.

'Oh, yes,' Candy said vaguely. 'Er—just let me write down when and where, Caroline.'

'Candy, I just told you! I do believe you're miles away!'

'I'm sorry. It's—there's a work problem that's been on my mind, and I'm afraid I did just find myself thinking over it again.'

'I'll write it on your calendar. If you don't mind?' Caroline fished out a pen from her handbag, and reached for Candy's wall calendar. 'February the third,' she said out loud. 'Caroline's engagement party.'

'I'll look forward to it, Caroline.'

'It should be a good do. Is there someone you'd like to bring, or will you be coming on your own?'

'I'll have to think about that.'

'You've broken up with Paul, I heard?'

'Not exactly. Really, it was never more than a friendship.'

'Oh? I must have misunderstood.'

Me too, Candy thought silently to herself. She had an urge to ask Caroline about Marshall, an urge to go on about him just as shamelessly as Caroline had been going on about James. But she knew that before she mentioned him to anyone, she would have to see him again and put things to rights between them.

Fifteen minutes later Caroline was gone, in a flurry of boisterous good spirits. Candy tipped their empty teacups into the sink, then she went slowly into her living-room, and picked up the telephone.

'Marshall?' she said, a moment later. 'You invited me to come and look at your photographs...'

CHAPTER TEN

MARSHALL must have been watching out for her; he had the front door open and was waiting for her on the steps when she got out of her car. Candy slammed the car door, and rushed across to join him.

'Hello, darling.'

'Hello, Candy.'

Her joy was so intense that it took her a moment to register the bleakness in his voice. He wouldn't meet her eyes. He was looking tired and drawn, with little lines around his eyes that she hadn't noticed before, etched clearly in the harsh light of the snowy day. This last week may have hurt me, Candy thought to herself, but it has hurt Marshall just as badly. And, unlike me, he doesn't yet know that the nightmare of misunderstandings is over.

'Can I come in?' she said gently.

'Yes, of course.' He moved aside to let her through the door, not touching her. 'You wanted to see my photos?'

'I wanted to talk, really. I mean, I do want to see your photos, of course I do, but they can wait.'

'Whatever you prefer. I've a fire lit downstairs.'

She followed him down the hallway and into the downstairs sitting-room. He had refurnished it, she noticed in passing, with a squashy sofa and chairs very similar to those she had chosen for her own living-room.

Blitzen looked up from where he was sprawled by the fire, but Candy barely noticed him. All her attention was fixed on Marshall.

'A drink? Sherry? Gin and tonic?'

'Anything.' She pulled off her gloves, then shrugged her winter coat off her shoulders and dropped it on the back of one of the chairs. Marshall was fixing their drinks. He wasn't looking at her. She watched him for a minute, pouring carefully with his back turned to her.

How tall he was, how elegant, how absolutely stunning. I never thought I would love and be loved by a man who looked like Marshall, she thought. But it wasn't only his looks that she loved, it was the man underneath. Not the handsome film-star image that was all some people saw of him, but the real man, with all his doubts and uncertainties, all his short temper and his perfectionism, his sudden bright smiles and his gentle gestures.

'You know you thought I was a real idiot when you first met me,' she said.

'I wouldn't put it quite like that.'

'Well, a bit of a scatterbrain.' She waited, but Marshall didn't reply, so she went on, hurriedly. 'I've something to tell you, and I guess it's going to make you think me even more of an idiot than you did then.'

Marshall dropped a slice of lemon into two gin and tonics and turned to her, with one in either hand.

Candy tried desperately to think of a sensible way of explaining, but she couldn't. So she said straight out, 'You see, to begin with, I thought you were Caroline's boyfriend...'

The gin and tonics wobbled, and she rushed forward to grab Marshall's hands and steady them.

'You what?' Marshall said in a low voice.

'Honest. I thought you were going out with Caroline Greenwood.'

'But Caroline's just got engaged to James Allen.'

'I know that now.' Candy grabbed one of the drinks and took a gulp. 'But for a horrible couple of days I actually thought she had got engaged to you.'

'I don't even *like* Caroline Greenwood!'

'Caroline's all right,' Candy said defensively. 'Look, I know it sounds stupid, Marshall, but I really did think it.'

'Since when?'

'Ever since I heard you and Caroline arguing outside my tent at the village fête.'

'Ever since you've known me!'

'Ever since.'

Marshall was staring at her in near incredulity. Candy gave him a tentative smile, and reached out to touch his cheek. 'I know it was idiotic of me,' she said unsteadily, 'but you see, I had this thing about tall blonde women. Andrew—the man I knew in London—left me for a tall blonde girl, and when I met you, and saw a tall blonde girl with you, I just assumed that you were as crazy about her as Andrew was about Georgina. Then Caroline told me about her wonderful boyfriend, and I didn't ask his name, and I never realised that the wonderful boyfriend wasn't you.'

'You really thought I'd got engaged to Caroline on Christmas Eve?'

'It made my New Year a bit bleak, I can tell you.'

'A bit bleak! Good God, you thought I'd got engaged to Caroline the day after I came round to your cottage!'

'I thought you were a thorough rotter, I can tell you!'

'Oh, Candy!'

'And now I know you're not,' Candy continued more brightly. 'So forgive me, please?'

'I still can't understand it.'

'I'll try to explain. But forgive me, please?'

She held Marshall's eyes, and saw a smile very slowly begin to spread across his face. 'I thought I'd lost you,' he said in a hoarse voice.

'Oh, no,' Candy whispered. 'You've only just found me.'

Much later, when the two of them were sitting—all but lying, really—on the sofa in front of his blazing fire, Marshall said thoughtfully, 'This house needs a family in it. I never used to get lonely back at the cottage, but here I have been. Except when you've been here.'

'Then I'll have to come here more often,' Candy murmured.

'Much more often.' He bent to kiss her forehead. 'I've always shied away from having steady girl-friends,' he continued. 'There have been a few, but it never looked like coming to anything. I always used to think I wouldn't ever get heavily involved with a woman. I thought I wouldn't marry, that it wasn't for me. My parents had such an unhappy marriage. I always said to myself that I wouldn't be like them, that I'd never have children myself in case they got to be as miserable as I was when I was a boy.'

'From the little I've heard,' Candy said gently, 'you're nothing like your parents.'

'I suppose not.' He met her eyes, and she looked steadily back into them. He doesn't even mind that I know, she thought with astonished gratitude. He's always kept the world at a very long distance, but now he's learning to change that—and fast. 'You're not like them either,' he added.

'Then our relationship won't be anything like theirs.'

'I'm sure it won't.' He kissed her again, and this time his lips continued their delicious exploration, tracing a slow path from temple to earlobe to the sensitive column of her neck.

'When did you change your mind?' Candy asked dreamily.

'About settling down?' Marshall raised his head. 'I honestly don't know. I wasn't consciously thinking about it when I bought this house, but then it seemed so large for just me, and I began to think how good it would be to fill it, and then I stumbled across this ridiculous girl who told my fortune.'

'Mutual attraction,' Candy murmured. 'Advantage in marrying.'

'Of course, it was all a load of rubbish.'

'Surprisingly accurate rubbish,' she retorted.

'Ah, but you don't know what my question was.'

So I don't, she thought. I guessed—and guessed hopelessly wrong at that! Now I know Marshall wouldn't have dreamed of asking about Caroline—but what would he have asked?

'What was it?'

'I'm not telling you that!'

'I want you to tell me everything,' she returned. 'All of it, Marshall. I want to know all about you from when you were a tiny boy, right through to who you are now. What you think, what you feel, what you're afraid of, what you enjoy.'

'I've never told anybody all of that.'

'You should.'

'Give me time and I will.' He yawned, and stretched his long body, snuggling down comfortably next to her. 'I *am* trying, Candy.'

'I know.' I won't push you too hard, she told herself. It's only a few weeks since you were too wary of loving to face up to developing our relationship. You would show some attraction and interest in me, then pull away fast, almost before I had a chance to respond to it. Then I thought it was Caroline that was making you hesitate, but now I know that there isn't another woman to be jealous of. There are only a few ghosts, fading in the sunshine of our love, that we shall learn to confront together.

'But that wretched question I'll never tell you, I warn you.'

'Why on earth not?'

'It might convince you the Oracle was right!'

Candy laughed, and kissed him lightly. 'I'm already convinced,' she retorted. 'There's no need for you to worry, though. I'll never use the Oracle again.'

'What, never?'

'No, never.' The Oracle may have tried to point me to you, she thought silently, but I read it so wrongly that instead it sent me in completely the opposite direction. If it hadn't been for that stupid Oracle and its mutual attraction, I might never have been so convinced that you belonged to Caroline.

'That's true love for you,' Marshall murmured. 'To give up your fortune-telling just to please me.'

'I'm not going to do what you tell me to do absolutely all the time.'

'I won't ask you to.'

'Are you sure?'

'Well, I'll try not to ask you to,' Marshall said.

Candy laughed, and after a moment he joined in, and they sat there in the firelight, laughing and loving together.

HARLEQUIN®
OFFICIAL SWEEPSTAKES RULES

NO PURCHASE NECESSARY

1. To enter, complete an Official Entry Form or 3"× 5" index card by hand-printing, in plain block letters, your complete name, address, phone number and age, and mailing it to: Harlequin Fashion A Whole New You Sweepstakes, P.O. Box 9056, Buffalo, NY 14269-9056.

   No responsibility is assumed for lost, late or misdirected mail. Entries must be sent separately with first class postage affixed, and be received no later than December 31, 1991 for eligibility.

2. Winners will be selected by D.L. Blair, Inc., an independent judging organization whose decisions are final, in random drawings to be held on January 30, 1992 in Blair, NE at 10:00 a.m. from among all eligible entries received.

3. The prizes to be awarded and their approximate retail values are as follows: Grand Prize — A brand-new Mercury Sable LS plus a trip for two (2) to Paris, including round-trip air transportation, six (6) nights hotel accommodation, a $1,400 meal/spending money stipend and $2,000 cash toward a new fashion wardrobe (approximate value: $28,000) or $15,000 cash; two (2) Second Prizes — A trip to Paris, including round-trip air transportation, six (6) nights hotel accommodation, a $1,400 meal/spending money stipend and $2,000 cash toward a new fashion wardrobe (approximate value: $11,000) or $5,000 cash; three (3) Third Prizes — $2,000 cash toward a new fashion wardrobe. All prizes are valued in U.S. currency. Travel award air transportation is from the commercial airport nearest winner's home. Travel is subject to space and accommodation availability, and must be completed by June 30, 1993. Sweepstakes offer is open to residents of the U.S. and Canada who are 21 years of age or older as of December 31, 1991, except residents of Puerto Rico, employees and immediate family members of Torstar Corp., its affiliates, subsidiaries, and all agencies, entities and persons connected with the use, marketing, or conduct of this sweepstakes. All federal, state, provincial, municipal and local laws apply. Offer void wherever prohibited by law. Taxes and/or duties, applicable registration and licensing fees, are the sole responsibility of the winners. Any litigation within the province of Quebec respecting the conduct and awarding of a prize may be submitted to the Régie des loteries et courses du Québec. All prizes will be awarded; winners will be notified by mail. No substitution of prizes is permitted.

4. Potential winners must sign and return any required Affidavit of Eligibility/Release of Liability within 30 days of notification. In the event of noncompliance within this time period, the prize may be awarded to an alternate winner. Any prize or prize notification returned as undeliverable may result in the awarding of that prize to an alternate winner. By acceptance of their prize, winners consent to use of their names, photographs or their likenesses for purposes of advertising, trade and promotion on behalf of Torstar Corp. without further compensation. Canadian winners must correctly answer a time-limited arithmetical question in order to be awarded a prize.

5. For a list of winners (available after 3/31/92), send a separate stamped, self-addressed envelope to: Harlequin Fashion A Whole New You Sweepstakes, P.O. Box 4694, Blair, NE 68009.

PREMIUM OFFER TERMS

To receive your gift, complete the Offer Certificate according to directions. Be certain to enclose the required number of "Fashion A Whole New You" proofs of product purchase (which are found on the last page of every specially marked "Fashion A Whole New You" Harlequin or Silhouette romance novel). Requests must be received no later than December 31, 1991. Limit: four (4) gifts per name, family, group, organization or address. Items depicted are for illustrative purposes only and may not be exactly as shown. Please allow 6 to 8 weeks for receipt of order. Offer good while quantities of gifts last. In the event an ordered gift is no longer available, you will receive a free, previously unpublished Harlequin or Silhouette book for every proof of purchase you have submitted with your request, plus a refund of the postage and handling charge you have included. Offer good in the U.S. and Canada only.

HOFW-SWPR

HARLEQUIN® OFFICIAL SWEEPSTAKES ENTRY FORM

4-FWHPS-4

Complete and return this Entry Form immediately – the more entries you submit, the better your chances of winning!

- Entries must be received by **December 31, 1991.**
- A Random draw will take place on **January 30, 1992.**
- No purchase necessary.

Yes, I want to win a FASHION A WHOLE NEW YOU Classic and Romantic prize from Harlequin:

Name ______________________ Telephone ______________ Age ________

Address ____

City ______________________ State ______________ Zip ______________

Return Entries to: **Harlequin FASHION A WHOLE NEW YOU,**
P.O. Box 9056, Buffalo, NY 14269-9056

PREMIUM OFFER

To receive your free gift, send us the required number of proofs-of-purchase from any specially marked FASHION A WHOLE NEW YOU Harlequin or Silhouette Book with the Offer Certificate properly completed, plus a check or money order (do not send cash) to cover postage and handling payable to Harlequin FASHION A WHOLE NEW YOU Offer. We will send you the specified gift.

OFFER CERTIFICATE

Item	A. ROMANTIC COLLECTOR'S DOLL (Suggested Retail Price $60.00)	B. CLASSIC PICTURE FRAME (Suggested Retail Price $25.00)
# of proofs-of-purchase	18	12
Postage and Handling	$3.50	$2.95
Check one	☐	☐

Name ____

Address ____

City ______________________ State ______________ Zip ______________

Mail this certificate, designated number of proofs-of-purchase and check or money order for postage and handling to: **Harlequin FASHION A WHOLE NEW YOU Gift Offer,** P.O. Box 9057, Buffalo, NY 14269-9057. Requests must be received by December 31, 1991.

ONE PROOF-OF-PURCHASE

4-FWHPP-4

To collect your fabulous free gift you must include the necessary number of proofs-of-purchase with a properly completed Offer Certificate.

See previous page for details.